A HinJew Story

A HINJEW STORY

Anita Samantaray Gavartin

ISBN 978-0-9884199-7-1

Library of Congress Control Number: 2012921066

For more information, please visit: www.ahinjewstory.com

Printed in the United States of America

To My Loving Husband

Acknowledgements

Grateful acknowledgement is made to all the HinJew couples in the world who embrace both the Hindu and Jewish traditions. My deep appreciation is extended to my parents, for all of their love and support through the years, and to my mentors, whose teachings were essential for this spiritual journey.

Contents

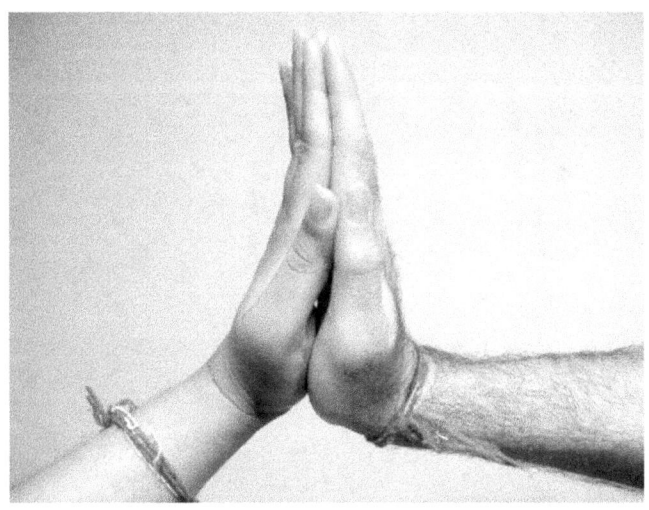

Introduction

"Mazel Tov!!" A HinJew is born. It was a fusion wedding between a daughter of East Indian Hindu immigrants and a son of Russian Jewish immigrants; one ceremony bringing together two of the oldest religions in the world. A HinJew may sound like the latest craze at an exotic restaurant but its definition is varied. It can be a person who is ½ Hindu and ½ Jewish, a Jewish person living in India, or it can be the union of a Hindu to a Jew. Shalom and Namaste, it works.

In this book, we explore the stories of a HinJew couple. HinJew couples face the same issues as every couple, in addition to those related to their different ethnic backgrounds. This is a story that illuminates the true spirit of love, which reaches beyond cultural differences and shows us just how similar we are. We live in an integrated world: When there is unrest in the Middle East, global oil prices rise. When Silicon Valley downsizes, engineers in India lose their jobs. Multicultural families face similar challenges; they must balance multiple moving variables to keep the peace.

HinJew couples are becoming more prevalent, and the stories of generations of HinJew children to come will be telling.

~1~

Salt and Pepper

"Like salt and pepper," described the delivery nurse.

Asha and Nina entered the world together. Asha was blessed with thick black hair and Nina's hair was golden blond. They were popular babies in the hospital due to their full heads of hair and became known as salt and pepper. Their mothers were friends, but having a newborn at home was hectic and so they did not see each other often, but they did keep in touch through Asha's and Nina's childhoods to some extent. Asha always thought of Nina as her oldest friend. They were born in the Bible Belt of the United States. Asha's parents could not assimilate to the South. "If you are not Christian, you are going to hell," their neighbors told them.

In 1969, Asha's father Akash had come to Boston from Kolkata, with eight dollars in his pocket. As the eldest son, he was the first in his family to become an engineer and to earn a scholarship to pursue a doctoral degree in materials science. It was a prosperous time to live in the U.S., Neil Armstrong had just landed on the moon, John Lennon of the Beatles released, "Give Peace a Chance" and Woodstock became an icon of hippie counterculture. Akash and his friends were full of optimism and had made big plans to change the world.

To his dismay, he worked for a professor who refused to grant him a degree. Asha's mother Jaya was also the eldest in her family. She was graceful and loved to study, and despite tradition she became a physician. When Jaya was in her final year of medical school, it was arranged for her to marry Akash. The two had only seen each other's photos and they met once, the day before their wedding. She completely trusted her father to choose a suitable mate for her. Jaya agreed to the marriage, and a month later moved to Boston. Was it marriage for love? Not exactly, it was love after marriage.

Meanwhile, Akash had accepted a job offer in Dallas. Akash excelled in the semiconductor industry, and Jaya had to work as a physician without compensation in order to gain U.S. experience. But their dreams prevailed and they both had successful careers.

One day, Asha came home from preschool singing, "Jesus loves me . . . oh, Jesus loves me," and after that the family headed to California. But the journey was not an easy one. Sometimes you have to suffer a real loss before you can feel joy. Sometimes you must leave everything behind to pursue a life of freedom.

California welcomed the family with open arms. The San Francisco Bay Area was a great place to raise a family. Asha followed in the footsteps of her mother, or so she tried. She loved the elderly and dreamt of becoming a neurologist. She loved the brain and its complexities. Asha studied neurobiology, physiology, and behavior, and was headed for medical school, just like her mother. After graduation, at the age of twenty, she was engaged to an Indian doctor, Rajiv or Raj for short.

It was a *pseudo*-arranged marriage. Both parents came from the same state in India, were Brahmins, and highly educated. On paper, their horoscopes lined up perfectly. "What is the exact time you were born?" asked the astrologer. Asha's family consulted an astrologer in India to make sure this was indeed an ideal match. "What city were you born in?" Astrology is a science, and algorithms are developed where you can input your data into a formula and it will tell you the future. Asha's parents believed in astrology.

But the unknown variable was Raj's temperament. He had a temper that went from one to ten in the blink of an eye, a temper that nobody knew about. They conducted a long-distance courtship and fell in love over the phone. It was only after Raj moved to San Francisco that Asha realized his nature, like a politician's, whose charm could only last so long until the truth is revealed.

One day, as part of their routine, Raj dropped by after work to Asha's place and they had dinner together. They began to discuss his residency applications and interviews and marriage. Asha said they would take one step at a time, and he snapped.

Raj grabbed Asha by her arms and then shook her vigorously. Her world turned black. The apartment was on the fifteenth floor and the window was slightly cracked open. She gasped for air. Later she thought in retrospect that if the window had been open wide enough, she should have pushed him through it. Instead he continued to shake her and threw her on the bed. She did not know what was happening, and all of a sudden Raj was on top of her. She could not block him and was forced to use her high school martial arts training. In one front kick, he flew across the room.

Asha was in disbelief that she hit the person she loved so much. How could this happen to her? She was a good person and always did the right thing. From this day forward, Asha would be on the defensive for the rest of her life, especially regarding men.

They hit rock bottom. An incident of physical and verbal abuse was reason enough to end the engagement. But she figured they could only go up from there and she gave Raj a second chance. She was embarrassed to tell her family, so decided not to and tried her best to make it work. She wished she could tell someone how she felt. Asha was the older sibling and felt compelled to complete the family's "formula" for her life. So the entire family flew to India for the wedding.

An American friend, Brooke, accompanied Asha and Raj; it was her first time to India. Brooke was Asha's best friend. She was an art history major and eager to see the sights of India, and there in front of the Taj Mahal, of all places, they encountered another episode of his anger.

The Taj Mahal is an ornate marble palace that was built by the Shah Jahan for his loving wife, Mumtaz. It is one of the finest examples of Mughal architecture, a style that combines elements from Indian, Persian, and Turkish architectural styles. It was evident that the Shah loved his wife.

Slum children followed Asha as they entered the grounds. She began to hand them spare coins. Raj lost it, again. "Why are you giving them money, they'll just keep following us," he yelled. "It's my money, what's it to you?" Asha fought back. Asha realized at that moment that she could not go on like this for the rest of her life. Did she really want to marry just for the sake of marrying? Was she doing this for her parents or for herself? Was she doomed to keep family tradition like her grandmother, mother, and aunts? Should she just internalize her feelings and keep silent as their mothers had taught them? Luckily for Asha, Brooke was there and gave her strength during this difficult time.

Asha was in tears and called her mother in Kolkata from the New Delhi airport, "Ma . . . ," she took a pause, trying to anticipate her mother's reaction, "the wedding is off." Asha knew she made the right choice. She had meditated the night before and asked God for a sign.

"Are you sure? But all the wedding prep is done. Come to Kolkata and we will talk about it," her mother said in a supportive tone of voice.

Asha could see the lines of anxiety forming on her mother's forehead, "Okay, I love you."

Her parents started a series of religious prayers to remove any evils spells that may have been cast upon the couple. Asha and company flew to meet her parents. The entire family greeted them at the airport and she could feel their love. As the wedding preparations were in full bloom, a "red-phone" meeting was quickly called between Asha and her parents as well as Raj and his parents.

The tension was high, so they met in a quiet corner of the Kolkata Botanical Garden. Every detail was laid out on the table, and a decision was made mutually to call off the wedding. In order to save face, the family told the public there was a death in the family. And they headed back to California. Raj pursued Asha for six months after that, but finally let it go. In the end, he found a girl online and married.

Asha underwent a total transformation. She was in the best shape of her life, tall, fair-skinned, with long black hair. But she was all emotion, on anti-depressants, and quickly started to gain weight. Her parents and the community, who once all loved her, did not know how to react. The community withdrew and it was if she did not exist. She felt like a ghost. When they did see her, they would say, "You've gained weight, but you look much happier." Asha began to realize how superficial the community was and questioned why her mother taught her to give so much importance to this community. All it cared about was status, where you lived, worked, etc. Asha felt suffocated and no longer wanted to live her life for someone else.

She would never view Indian men in the same way again. Her father is traditional and her brother the other extreme, completely ignoring his Indian identity. She loved them dearly, but could never relate to them. Instead, she decided to do her own research. She wanted to see how other men from different cultures would treat women. Asha went on a rampage: dating Japanese men, European men, and many others. She made a decision to enjoy this time and to rewrite the formula for her happiness.

She was no longer in a rush to marry, and if she never married at all that was okay, too. Whether she was single or married, it did not matter to her. And if she did decide to marry, it had to be with the right person. Asha had made a decision. If she did not find the right person, she would not marry.

She didn't care about status or salary; she just wanted to find a good human being. Someone you want to hug at the end of the day. Someone you can laugh with and love. Every two years since Asha was a child, she had traveled to India with her family. Only her immediate family lived in the U.S., the rest lived in India and Europe. This biennial trip would make for great vacations, but she always longed for a large family, thus she was attracted to Latin and Jewish cultures.

Asha was an independent woman. She was a Division Manager at a prestigious university. She had purchased her own home at the age of twenty-five. In fact, many men couldn't handle her independence. Asha didn't need men, nor did she want to be in a relationship, but she did want to have her own family. The problem was, if a man started to get close, she pushed him away. She was also approaching the age of thirty, far too old by Indian standards. Asha traveled the world: to Africa, Asia, Australia, Europe, and South America. It occurred to her to ask herself: Did she enjoy travelling or was she just running away from her problems? She had learned so much about people and now she viewed the world through her travels.

"Habibti, you must be with me," said her Egyptian scuba diver instructor.

"I just want to dive. Can you take me on a dive?" she asked.

"Yes, but only if I can take you to dinner afterwards."

"Where?"

"We can go somewhere close the hotel."

"Okay, deal." They agreed.

Asha was an avid scuba diver, which added la crème to her vacations. She had finished a tour in Egypt and extended her stay to Sharm El Sheikh. At the time, it was on orange alert as there had been terrorist bombings a few months back. She figured: Would they really bomb the same city twice? Asha decided to take a risk only to scuba dive in the Red Sea. The Red Sea was not actually red. It was three shades of blue and teal, like waters of fantasy resorts on the covers of travel magazines. Asha saw barracudas and beautifully colored ray-finned fish that could only be found in the Middle East.

The problem soon became her scuba diver buddy, Ali. Ali worked in the dive shop in the hotel she was staying at. Wherever Asha went, be it South America, India, or Egypt, she was able to blend in with the locals. Ali would not take no for an answer, so Asha informed the hotel manager that she would be having dinner in a nearby restaurant with him. She did not go far, but was able to see Egypt from the locals' perspective. Cairo, the Nile, and

Alexandria have lots to offer, but for a tourist the best experiences are when you mingle with the locals. Nightlife in Sharm El Sheikh is spare, so Asha was lucky to spend time with Ali and his friends. She then continued on to Israel.

"Where are you coming from?" asked the El Al agent.

"Egypt."

"What were you doing in Egypt?"

"I was on a tour."

"And you are going to Israel by yourself?"

"I'm going to visit a friend in Rehovat."

"What friend? Where did you meet him?"

"At a party, sorry—I meant in San Francisco."

"Does he speak Hebrew?

"Yes, and also Russian."

"What is his phone number?" the agent continued.

"His name is Pasha and here is his number."

"Hmm," he studied the phone number. "I will call, please wait here."

Asha answered all of the El Al agent's questions and barely made the one-hour flight from Cairo to Tel Aviv. They tested, scanned, wiped, and retested all luggage items, especially the electronics. Given Israel's history, it's understandable that they have tight security, but to take a hair straightener away? That was crossing the line. Asha simply wanted to visit the "holy city" of Jerusalem and happened to have a few friends living in Rehovat, near Hebrew University.

Asha walked the streets of Jerusalem, one of the oldest cities in the world. Pasha drove her through the Judean Mountains, between the Mediterranean Sea and the northern edge of the Dead Sea. They hiked the Masada trails and floated in the Dead Sea. Asha tried to swim, but the water was dense with salt. It was green, with white salt crystal formations on the edges of the rocks, and known to heal wounds.

The next stop was Jerusalem, home to the three major Abrahamic religions—Judaism, Christianity, and Islam. As Asha walked through the city, she encountered the pristine Jewish quarters that were rebuilt after being destroyed (twice), the clearly marked Muslim quarters, and the church-filled Christian quarters. You could feel the history and each sector's pride. People wore the look of survival on their faces.

As a Hindu, Asha for the first time in her life felt like a real tourist. Near the Wailing Wall, there were circles of Hasidic Jews reading from the Torah, and lines of Israeli soldiers, male and female, with their guns. Asha made a joke and asked if she could have a photograph taken of her with gun in hand, with the soldiers. They weren't supposed to, but agreed. It seemed wrong to be carrying guns in such a spiritual place. But after all when you live in Israel, you live as if it could be your last day.

~2~

Ladki Meets Latke

Asha drove to San Francisco on a Wednesday night after work to meet Alon, a friend visiting from Los Angeles. By habit, a group of Alon's friends were gathered at a Moroccan lounge downtown. As Asha and Svetlana were waiting for Alon's arrival, a gentleman entered the room and saw two beautiful black eyes, and said to the girl:

"Hola, hablas español?" he asked.

"Sí, yo hablo," Asha responded.

Asha's roommate in college was Russian, so she had met quite a few Russians. But this was the first time she was meeting Ilya. He had traveled extensively throughout South America and was able to impress Asha with his Spanish. He thought Asha looked Latina, but could not place her. They carried on an entire conversation in Spanish. Asha ended with, "By the way, I'm Indian," and Ilya said, "By the way, I'm Russian!" Asha smiled and whispered to Svetlana, "He's thin, but seems sweet."

On their first date, Ilya picked up Asha from her parent's house. He built up his nerves as he rang the doorbell. What was he going to say to the father? "You have a beautiful daughter?" "What a lovely house?" Questions pounded through his head and stories of Ghandi and his Salt March.

Akash, Asha's father, answered the door.

As he opened the door, the earth shook, literally. According to the local news, there was an earthquake of magnitude 4.2 on the Richter scale. Just the icebreaker he needed. In fact, when Ilya's family had arrived in California there was a similar earthquake two weeks later.

During his first earthquake, Vadim, Ilya's father, was on a job interview. He barely knew English, and on top of that had to run for his life and hide under a table. He thought the building would collapse on him.

This was a perfect situation to introduce himself into Asha's family: "Talk about *welcome* to America," said Ilya, and dazzled them with his charm and smile.

Spanish cuisine was a great choice for that evening's restaurant. The two dipped into various tapas dishes. But the main dish, paella, a Valencian rice dish, was Asha's favorite. Flamenco guitar music was playing in the background, and the sangria was sweet with fresh nectarines, thinly sliced peeled ginger, and pears.

After dinner, Ilya had a surprise for Asha. He drove her to a small café, but it was closed. "I don't see any lights on," remarked Asha. "Trust me—I'll be back in a minute." As Asha waited in the car, the lights of the café turned on and Ilya let her in. "How did you do that?" Asha didn't know that Ilya had been the manager of this café in high school and still had a spare key. "Would you like a drink?" he asked. "No, it's okay," said Asha. Ilya looked at Asha in disappointment. "Ah, okay, I'll take a white chocolate mocha." Ilya turned on the coffee machine, and Asha.

Months went by: Asha did not have time for a serious relationship. She was immersed in her work, friends, and community service. She did however meet with Ilya a few times, and then more frequently. After seeing her mother being emotionally battered by her father's ill treatment and pettiness all her life, it became hard for her to believe in love. Her mother made a decision to put the community before her own happiness. But Asha wanted to do the opposite.

Ilya planned to attend an International Society of Molecular Biology conference in Rio de Janeiro. For some trips, he was able to bring along a significant other. He decided to take a risk and ask Asha.

"Asha, would you like to go to Brazil with me?"

"I don't even know you," she hesitated. Normally, she would date a man for at least a year before accepting such an offer.

"Hey, I think it's a pretty good offer, don't you?" he asked.

"Yes, if you know the person," she said.

It was flattering, but Asha was not ready to let her guard down. A bit forward for only knowing a person for a few months, but Ilya persisted. Asha learned that when men want something, they let you know.

Ilya suddenly remembered Sofia from Argentina. If Asha said no, maybe he could meet her in Rio? Before Ilya met Asha, he was in love with Sofia.

She was Latina, provided a private tour of the city, her uncle's house, and was half Jewish. In fact, on his first date with Asha, Sofia was all he could think about. He compared Asha to Sofia and was in love with the idea of love. But it was a travel romance with Sofia, that's all. When Ilya came to know the truth about Sofia, that she was in fact one hundred percent Catholic, that chapter was closed. It was not her religion that bothered him, but the fact that she had lied to him.

Ilya attended the Rio conference on his own. Instead of contacting his past love, he went paragliding with his colleagues. He wanted to experience flight in its purist form over the Tijuca National Park, the largest urban rainforest in the world. It is considered the best spot in Brazil for tandem flights. Ilya was a risk taker.

Ilya continued to pursue Asha. They both loved to travel and went to Mexico and Canada together. But Ilya wanted them to see the world together. He wanted to show Asha where he was born and raised, the lake where he learned to swim, the summerhouse that his grandfather built with his own hands, all in Russia.

Asha had lived in Italy for six months and saw most of the countries in Western Europe, but had yet to see Eastern Europe. One sport they both obsessed about was *fútbol* (soccer). Before Italy, Asha had never watched a game of soccer, but Europeans are crazy for it. Adult men cry during a game, blood pressure and adrenalin rise, you hug and kiss the fans seated next to you, it is an out-of-body experience.

"How about going to South Africa for the World Cup?" Ilya suggested.

"Isn't it hard to get tickets?" asked Asha.

"You leave that up to me, I'll take care of it."

Asha was not used to this kind of generosity. With Russian men, you leave your wallet at home. They open the doors for you, pay for your meals, and plan your vacations. It was all new to Asha. Not to say that Indian men cannot be generous, but "well-mannered" is culturally relative. In Indian culture (and many others), burping after a meal is a sign of satisfaction and a compliment to the host.

"Sure, let's do South Africa—I've always wanted to go on a safari," she hinted.

"Great, consider it done," Ilya said with confidence.

South Africa is similar to California, except that you drive on the opposite side of the road. Many countries doubted its ability to host the World Cup. But South Africa came out on top, through patience and perseverance. Asha and Ilya were lucky to win tickets through a lottery system online. And with that, the planning started.

It was like planning a wedding; everything was triple the price. Johannesburg or Jo-burg as the locals call it was not of particular interest, but they really cleaned up the city for World Cup. Asha and Ilya were to fly into Cape Town and leave from Jo-burg. Their itinerary included: the wine lands, safari, and World Cup games.

Ilya supported Argentina, but Asha loved Italia. "Forza Italia! Viva Argentina!" yelled the fans painted in blue and white. At a local fan fest, Asha and Ilya also painted their faces in honor of Messi and Maradona, the superpowers of fútbol.

Their friendship turned to love. Ilya came from a large Jewish family, a family anybody would be lucky to be part of, from great grandparents to grandchildren. Asha met them all. It was clear that they were not expecting someone like her; after all she is not Jewish. But when she met the grandmother, Babushka pulled Ilya aside and said, "Ah, she's beautiful and looks Israeli." Ilya asked Babushka,

"Did you ever think I would date a shiksa?" Shiksa is a Yiddish term for a white, non-Jewish, girl. "I don't think she qualifies as a shiksa, let's call her Induska (an Indian girl in Russian)."

Ilya felt pressure to carry on the family name and in order for his children to be Jewish, the mother had to be Jewish. Similar beliefs are shared in Indian culture. More than ninety percent of Hindus are married to other Hindus. But, when you find love, you do not see race, creed, or gender. You see the human being for who s/he is and that is what counts. When someone brings out the best in you, you know it's right. Asha and Ilya connected on the world level.

Asha's grandfather had once told her, "Everyone has positive and negative attributes. Always look at the positive and you will be happy." When you are inherently negative, this can be hard to do. When you have been hurt, it is understandable that you will have difficulty trusting again. One builds a ring of protection that can take decades to break down. Luckily for Asha, Svetlana had led her to Ilya.

Their love turned into marriage. It happened so quickly. She wasn't sure how exactly, but it happened. When it's your time, everything falls in place. Sometimes the most important decisions in life happen in a flash. Asha and Ilya had both a traditional Hindu ceremony and a Jewish ceremony. They liked to call it their HinJew ceremony. The program included:

Hindu Ceremony

Var Agaman & Ganesha Puja
Ilya arrives escorted to the mandap by his family and friends, and is received by Asha's parents, Akash and Jaya. This purification ceremony begins with a prayer to Lord Ganesha, who is the remover of all obstacles and symbolizes truth, friendship, and happiness.

Bride's Welcome & Jai Mala

Surrounded by her bridal party, Asha is escorted to the mandap (canopy). Asha and Ilya then exchange garlands, showing their mutual acceptance as future husband and wife.

Kanyadaan & Haatha Ganthi

Asha's parents give the bride away for marriage by placing Asha's hands into Ilya's. Ilya symbolically accepts his responsibility to love, respect, and protect her forever.

Granthi Bandhan

To symbolize their union, the loose ends of the bride and groom's garments are tied together by Elena, Ilya's sister, and Anushka, Asha's cousin, in a matrimonial knot symbolizing a firm and lasting commitment.

Havan

Agni, the Lord of Fire, blesses the couple with purity and happiness as the flame is lit.

Mangal Phera

Asha and Ilya walk around a sacred fire seven times. The first four rounds represent life's four elements: *Dharma* (Duty), *Artha* (Wealth), *Kama* (Love and Family), and *Moksha* (Salvation). The last three rounds represent *Gunas* (Moods): *Satogun* (Purity), *Rajogun* (Passion), and *Tamogun* (Inertia).

Saptapadi

The couple takes seven steps around the fire, symbolic of the seven steps of life. With each step, the couple takes a vow and asks for God's blessings as they strive to fulfill the principal duties of married life.

Sindoor Daan & Ring Exchange

Ilya fills the parting of Asha's hair with sindoor (vermillion), which signifies that she is now married.

Kansarbhoj
The bride and groom feed one another sweets, signifying their total commitment to each other.

Sala Bidha
Arun, the bride's brother, gives Ilya a pat on the back as a reminder to take care of his sister!

Akhand Saubhagyavati
Married women in the family whisper blessings and secrets in the bride's ear.

Lajja Vastra
Ilya's parents, Vadim and Diana, give the bride a new dress to shower her with their blessings.

Ashrivaad
The priest and family bless the newly married couple. The newlyweds then ask their parents, family, and friends for their blessings.

Jewish Ceremony

Ketubah
Prior to the ceremony, Asha and Ilya signed a document called Ketubah. This is the Jewish marriage contract. This document, written in Hebrew, is read by the Rabbi during the ceremony.

Chuppah
The wedding is held under a chuppah or "canopy" in Hebrew. This canopy is a symbol of the home that the new couple will build together. The bride circles the groom seven times.

The Kiddushin

The ceremony begins with a blessing over wine, a traditional Jewish symbol of simcha (joy). The couple shares their first cup of wine, symbolic of the simchot they will share in their marriage. Then the couple exchanges rings.

Sheva Brachot

The second part of the ceremony consists of the recitation of Sheva Brachot, seven blessings. The blessings are for Asha and Ilya as individuals and as beloved companions united in joy and gladness, laughter and song, love and harmony, peace and friendship.

Breaking the Glass

The couple drinks from the cup of wine and Ilya breaks a glass with his foot. A broken glass cannot be mended; likewise the promises made by the couple are irrevocable. The glass is broken to protect the marriage, "As this glass shatters, so may our marriage never break."

Yichud

After Asha and Ilya leave the chuppah, they spend a few minutes alone in isolation known as yichud. These few moments will give the couple an opportunity to recognize the sanctity of their new life together.

Mazel Tov!!

It had been a beautiful day on the shores of Half Moon Bay, California. A dozen pelicans flew over the mandap (canopy), as family and friends had gathered to celebrate this union. The couple walked along a rose-petal path, as the fathers put their hands into each other's.

Two became one. Two religions, two cultures, became one. "The word Brahmin comes from the word Abraham," said the Rabbi. Apparently, Jesus traveled to India and incorporated Hindu principals into Christianity as well. Religion is personal, and Asha and Ilya did not let it divide them. In fact, they adopted philosophies from both religions into their own. So, the spiritual journey began.

During the first year of marriage, Asha and Ilya decided to keep a HinJew home. They introduced themselves to the home, one room at a time. In the living room they had their ketubah, the Jewish marriage contract written in Hebrew signed by their Rabbi and Hindu priest. Next to it, a modern hamsa hand, also common in Middle Eastern cultures. Asha purchased it in Tel Aviv during her first trip to Israel before she knew Ilya; it was a work of art. The hand is protection from the evil eye or evil spirits. In their temple, they placed Hindu deities as well as Jewish signs. All shared common symbolism and meaning in their lives.

Asha learned transcendental meditation with her family in an ashram in New Delhi at the age of ten. Imagine rows of orange-draped, bald monks in deep meditation. It was a Zen moment. When she saw her guru levitate before her eyes, she was sold. In meditation, you can completely separate your mind from your body, as your mind transcends to different levels of consciousness. You cannot feel your body, it is numb, your heart rate is lowered and you breathe in a rhythmic pattern. Your state of mind is at peace. It is the most relaxing feeling in the world and takes just five minutes, once trained. Ideally, five minutes in the morning and five minutes before you sleep. It was there Asha had come to learn about her own spirituality.

Yes, she'd been to hundreds of temples all over the world, but the real temple was within. This is the concept she wanted to practice with her family. Sure, it's great celebrating so many holidays: Chanukah, Rosh Hashanah, Yom Kippur, Diwali, Holi, and loads of pujas (Hindu rituals). But religion is a way of life. Whether you believe in a religion or not, we all seek something better and to be better. Asha questioned religion, was it really about reciting prayers? Or was it about the family coming together to spend quality time with each other? Family time was important to both Asha and Ilya.

Ilya's spiritual journey was that of transcendental hesitation. He practiced meditation alone and with Asha, but often fell asleep.

He also attempted to read the Kabbalah, but in the end preferred logic. The Kabbalah defines the nature of the universe and human beings, the nature and purpose of existence, and various ontological questions to help attain spiritual realization. The Torah (Jewish holy book) also includes many stories of mystical experiences, from visitations by angels to prophetic dreams and visions. World-reknowned Rabbis have visited the Dalai Lama in the mountains of India to exchange secrets. And mysticism is also integral to both Judaism and Hinduism.

Asha took a closer look at tantric traditions and the concept of *chakras* (centers of energy) in her Reiki class in San Francisco. At the beginning of each class, the students sat in a circle, and meditated focusing on the energy flow from the top of the head, to the heart, to the base of the spine. She learned that the seven chakras were connected to major organs and glands: *Sahasrara* (crown), *Ajna* (brow), *Vishudda* (throat), *Anahata* (heart), *Manipura* (solar plexus), *Swadhisthana* (sacral), *Muladhara* (root). The flow of energy to these junctions can create healing effects on the body.

Similarly, the Kabbalah states that everything in the spiritual world takes place through the medium of the *Sefirot*. Just as the Vedas describe the chakras as wheels of light, the Kabbalah describes the Sefirot as cosmic forces in nature. The names of the ten Sefirot are: *Chochmah* (wisdom), *Binah* (understanding), *Daat* (knowledge), *Chessed* (kindness), *Gevurah* (strength), *Tiferet* (beauty), *Netzach* (victory), *Hod* (splendor), *Yesod* (foundation), and *Malchut* (kingship). The ten Sefirot are generally divided into two categories: *Sechel* (intellect) and *Middot* (emotions). It is believed that these are the stages one must go through to reach the divine. Ilya had developed emotional intelligence at a young age, but Asha struggled with hers.

Asha and Ilya often visited the mountains to refresh their spirit. This helped them reconnect with the peace and adopt their own HinJew principles: to lead a moral life, to be kind to others, to practice self-control, to be mindful and aware of your thoughts and actions. In fact, such principles are common in every religion and culture, to act for the welfare and happiness of all beings, to be generous, to speak the truth, and to care for the mind and body.

~3~

Bombay to Goa

A wise man once said, "If you want to know yourself, travel alone, and if you want to learn about someone else, travel with them." After their first year of marriage, Asha and Ilya decided to go to India together. "This year, we'll visit my family and next year we can visit yours," she explained, "I have five cousins in London and usually try to route my trips through London, is that okay?" she asked. "Sure, no problem," Ilya said enthusiastically.

Traveling as a married couple, everything was new again. Asha found herself taking extra caution; planning a little more extensively than if she was traveling with her parents. They took all the preventive measures and were fully immunized. Asha was in contact with all of her relatives to prepare them for Ilya's arrival; after all, he was a new member to the family. In fact, they were to have a small reception to formally introduce him.

First stop, London Heathrow. It was cold and snowing outside and Asha was in true form sporting her flip-flops. Not a problem, since her cousin Sarita was to pick them up in her car and drive them to her flat in North London, the meeting place where all the cousins would reunite from time to time. It was a festive time in London as the city was in preparation for the summer Olympics. The streets were lined with international flags as if walking through a UN convention. They only had an overnight stay in London, but at least they were able to meet Sarita's new daughter.

When they arrived, Asha went upstairs to freshen up, and a lovely Indian meal greeted Ilya. Asha ate on the flight, so she started with the sweets. It was a family trait, to love sweets. They talked and talked. Asha did not sleep; she played with her niece and enjoyed every minute. It dawned on her—she worked all year so she could take one month off to visit family. It was worth every moment. Even though her cousins lived in the UK, she felt very close to them.

Next stop, Bombay, or as it's now called, Mumbai. Mumbai is the Los Angeles of India. Pinto, Asha's cousin Seema's driver, greeted them. Pinto was dressed smartly in a pressed shirt and slacks, and was the best driver she knew. Ilya appreciated that Asha's family treated their workers well. Driving in India is chaotic, people don't follow rules, and there are no lanes. In India, you create your own lane. Most middle-class families in India have their own drivers; it's the only way to get around unless you are in New Delhi where they have introduced a metro system. Pinto was to pick them up from the airport, then go collect Seema from work, her daughter, Mamali, from school, and drive them to Pune to attend another cousin's wedding reception.

On the way, Mamali asked Ilya many questions. She was dressed in a school uniform and wearing the cutest pair of glasses. "How come you have an accent?"

Ilya smiled at her.

"Where did you come from?" she continued.

"We're from California, do you know California?" replied Ilya.

"I know California, California Pizza Kitchen!" she said. They laughed for hours. Mumbai only has one California Pizza Kitchen and it happens to be near her school.

During the drive to Pune, Seema checked her Facebook account for the address.

Asha mentioned to her, by the way, did you ever accept Ilya's friend request? She said, no because I didn't know his last name. "Sorry, I get so many friend requests from random people," Seema said.

"I understand, I still get invited to join, but I haven't caved in yet," exclaimed Asha.

With a push of a button, Ilya and Seema became friends. Thirty minutes later, Seema gets a phone call:

"Are you Seema?"

"Yes."

"Do you work for BBC?" Seema was taken aback.

"Excuse me, who is this?" she asked.

"Do you know Ilya Zalan?" the gentleman persisted.

"Yes, and who is calling?"

"Ilya has my bag."

"Okay, we are driving to Pune; can we call you back tomorrow?"

"Sorry—this is urgent, you have my suitcase." There was an awkward silence.

"Wait a minute; first tell me, how did you get my number?"

"Listen, how long will you be in Pune?" the man asked.

"We are returning to Bombay tomorrow and can meet you at the airport in the afternoon, does that work for you?"

"Yes, let's meet at 2:00 p.m."

"Sorry, what's your name again?" The gentleman hung up the phone abruptly.

When they arrived at Pune, they checked the bag carefully but found no nametags. Should they have opened it? They weren't sure what to do and left it in the car. Her parents who had arrived two weeks earlier and her aunts and uncles joined Asha.

Well-wishers greeted the couple with garlands, and Ilya and Asha joined in by throwing rose petals. It was a December wedding, with a serene, outdoor reception.

On the return from Pune, they met Amit Ghandi at the Bombay airport to exchange bags. An officer accompanied Mr. Ghandi at the airport.

"It was because of you this man went through a lot of misery," shouted the officer.

"Sorry for taking your bag, they looked exactly the same."

"You don't understand I need my oats," said Mr. Ghandi.

"Your oats?" Good thing it wasn't something else, thought Ilya, or they would have spent their vacation in jail. "Do you want to check and make sure this is your bag?" asked Ilya.

"Come with us, you must sign some documents, this is his bag," said the officer.

Asha was frightened as the officer took Ilya and Mr. Ghandi to the customs office for thirty minutes. She was asked to wait outside with Pinto. How long would it take? They had to catch a flight to Goa in two hours. Forty minutes went by and Asha was getting more and more curious about what was inside the suitcase. She combed her fingers through her hair frantically, and contemplated, who was this Amit Ghandi and how did he obtain Seema's contact information?

Finally, Ilya walked out of the departure gate with their suitcase in hand. Asha was relieved, and Ilya was excited to catch his flight to Goa. There was no sign of Mr. Ghandi.

The couple continued on to travel through India exploring one town at a time, Mumbai, Goa, Jaipur, Udaipur, etc. It was like the beginning of their relationship. Each city is different, as is each stage in a relationship. Each has its own personality, traits, and you can learn something about yourself. They posted photos on Facebook so their family and friends could track them.

Asha took the time to capture the food, colors, and smells of India in her photos. Asha loved Udaipur, sipping tea every morning from their balcony that overlooked Lake Pichola. Udaipur is the city of lakes and palaces and capital of the Rajasthan province. Palaces have been converted into hotels, and Asha and Ilya felt like royalty during their stay. You can still feel the history of the Mughal Empire in the air.

After two weeks of traveling, Ilya fell sick, "ugh, my stomach," he cried. Ilya was moaning and groaning and felt very uncomfortable. "Babychka, are you okay?" asked Asha. "Maybe you're just nervous to meet the family?" she thought seriously. And with that Ilya ran to the toilet and vomited the 9,000 rupee meal they had shared at the Taj

Rambagh Palace. "I don't think that's me being nervous," exclaimed Ilya.

"Do you want to try on a lungi? Maybe you'll feel more comfortable," Asha suggested.

"What's a lungi?"

"Try it on . . . I bought some in Goa for my uncle."

"What I need is a diaper!" exclaimed Ilya. Asha was amazed at how Ilya could turn any situation into humor, and that's why she loved him.

A lungi, also known as a sarong, is a traditional garment worn around the waist in Indonesia, India, Sri Lanka, Burma, Malaysia, and Singapore—to name a few places. It is particularly popular in regions where the heat and humidity create an unpleasant climate for briefs, and it can be tied in a simple knot. Asha tried to comfort Ilya. It was their last night in Jaipur just before they were to go to Bengal to meet the family and attend their reception.

It was nice to have some leisure time to relax with the family after all their traveling in India. Even though it was far from home, they felt comfortable because the family treated Ilya like their own. Asha and Ilya were pampered and fed five meals a day. Teatime was Asha's favorite time of day and where she was able to chat with her grandmother and mother, three generations alone together. It was a lazy two weeks, but since Asha's parents were the eldest, and Asha and her brother their eldest children, they were highly respected in the larger family group. In Indian culture, you do not argue with your elders. Even if you may differ in opinion, you do not say a word, out of respect. Not to mention, as one of the elders you can boss them around. When was the last time a cousin of yours massaged your feet? It was a luxury.

The day of the reception arrived and it felt like a second wedding. After a dose of antibiotics, Ilya had started to feel better. He was to wear traditional Indian clothes and Asha planned to wear the sari that her mother-in-law gifted her on her wedding day. She carried it in her backpack halfway around the world for this very special day. Ilya's parents didn't have the vacation days and were unable to join them in India, so at least they would see that Asha wore their sari in the photos. She wanted to include them somehow.

The couple was greeted by dozens of family members. "Asha, do you remember me? I taught you yoga," said an uncle, or "Remember me, we used to collect crabs on the beach?" asked another cousin. Family members lined up, shook their hands, took a photo, and the assembly line continued throughout the night. "Ilya, nice to meet you, how is your stomach?" they all asked. News travels quickly in an Indian family. But they were genuinely concerned asking Ilya about his health and bowel movement, a good introduction to the family.

The next morning they opened gifts and decided to donate everything to Asha's favorite orphanage. Imagine eighty children living in two rooms. They need infrastructure and survive on 10,000 rupees (roughly $200) a month. Two years before, she had purchased fifteen bicycles for the children so they could ride to school instead of walking miles. She worked in partnership with Indians to develop sustainable models to enhance the quality of life and resilience of rural areas through health improvements and education.

It was a place she visited every time she was in Kolkata and she wanted to show Ilya. Social workers operate it with no government assistance. On their way, they stopped at a store to buy some chocolates. Ilya handed each child one piece of chocolate. It was a small gesture, but a real treat for the children. They do not even have enough toilets or beds and literally have to sleep shoulder-to-shoulder.

It was privately funded by donations and somehow survived. One child was special (had Down syndrome). Asha met her as a baby when she was found in a garbage bin, at the time she had just passed her medical clearance. Two years later, the baby had grown into a beautiful girl.

She was late to arrive, but when she did, Ilya handed her a chocolate. The girl did not know that the others had already received their chocolates. But she took her one piece and divided it into three pieces to share with her two friends. Ilya was amazed how these children with so little were able to be so happy.

"We are so lucky, thank you for sharing this with me," Ilya said to Asha. Ilya knew this was a special place for Asha and felt closer to Asha by visiting the orphanage. It was an experience that he would remember always, and even though they were orphaned, it seemed that the children were happy to be with each other. Even the poorest of the poor are so giving in India. They seem content and are not greedy. They do not try to steal from others, and have accepted the reality of their situation and live with it. They figure there is somebody else in a worse situation.

Asha was humbled by India every time she visited. Ilya's eyes also opened a little wider. They realized that they were part of a world community, and when people communicate with and understand each other they create a better world.

~4~

Tortellini vs. Pelmeni

In a free society, the communication of ideas, on a large or small scale, and in any tongue, plays a vital role in shaping the life of every individual. Asha found that the key in mastering any language was to practice speaking it.

"Ten dolla, ten dolla . . . San Francisco t-shirts for only ten dolla," repeated the merchant.

"Hola, señor. Por favor, tres para veinte dolares?" Asha bargained.

"No, I can't. I have big boss señorita."

"Okay, gracias."

"Un momento, you eh-speak Spanish?"

"Sí, entonces, veinte y cuatro dolares?" asked Asha.

"Veinte y cinco, está bien?" he asked.

"Sí, está bien," she agreed to the deal: three t-shirts for twenty-five dollars.

Asha had studied Spanish since the seventh grade. She spoke the most Spanish when translating for others. Often, she would translate for her parents, who joked around that they did not know the difference between Spanish and French. Her parents' construction workers could only speak Spanish, so any time the workers needed further instructions the orders were filtered through Asha. Without her ability to speak Spanish, her family might be misunderstood. Asha's passion for language had led her to Siena, Italy.

Asha participated in the Education Abroad Program at the Universitá per Stanieri di Siena. She studied Italian culture and language during her last semester in college. "Buongiorno. Benvenuti alla classe italiana. In questa classe ci sarà solo parlare in italiano, non in inglese," said the professor on the first day of class. Asha was terrified, she did not know a word of Italian, but she knew how to speak Spanish, how different could it be? she thought. It was very different. Both languages are Latin-based, but grammatically different.

Studying abroad was the best decision of her life. It was the first time she was away from home and she was able to immerse herself in a different culture. Her mother warned her about Italian men and that they would want to marry her. But Asha was not there for the men. She watched soccer games, traveled to major Italian cities on the weekends, and learned Italian cooking. Until one day, when she met Gabrielli Cafarelli, or Cafa for short. She was enamored of him.

Cafa worked in a bank and would exchange Asha's dollars into Italian lire. She spoke to him every day and quickly picked up the Italian language. It is the best way to learn a language really, to get a boyfriend. But Cafa was more than a boyfriend to Asha. Some relationships have no name. All she knew was she could never bring him home to her parents. It is true that Italians love women. And Asha loved Italians. But Asha soon discovered that these grown men lived at home with their mothers and did not get married.

Many romanced her. Asha learned about herself, love, and men. It was the happiest time of her life. Every morning she walked to the local mercato to buy fresh produce, walked to class, worked out, and cooked in the dormitory. Students came from all over the world—a Japanese chef who came to learn Italian cooking, another group from Hungary—all in all there were seventy-five students living together for the common purpose of learning the Italian language. Friendships formed and life was bella (beautiful).

****

Life is so stressful in the U.S. It took Asha only a day to realize that when she returned from abroad with Ilya. Her body and soul were so much happier when she was outside the hustle and bustle of Silicon Valley; she rarely wanted to return. Asha was restless. She could never sit still, and as soon as she was back from one trip, she was busy planning the next. Their next trip together was St. Petersburg, Russia. Ilya had not visited since he left as a child.

Ilya was nine years old when he emigrated from Russia. He thought he was going on a vacation to America, but when he saw his mother Diana crying he knew something did not add up. She spent days cleaning the apartment and packed all their belongings into two suitcases for four people. A total of eight would travel together, Vadim and his family and his sister's family. It was during the Soviet regime and President Gorbachev opened the gates for Jews to move to Israel. Ilya's family was granted visas to leave the Soviet Union for Israel. But the plan was to land in America. Ilya's grandmother's older brother Isaac had gone to America during the first wave of Jewish refugees; Ilya's family would be the second wave.

The family missed their train to Austria, so they re-routed to Poland for a day. They were to spend two and a half weeks in Vienna in order to apply for American visas. A choice had to be made—Israeli, Australian, or American visas—they chose the latter. But, sponsorship to California took months. In some cases, families would have to wait six months to a year.

A nonprofit company organized the effort through Italy. The family found comfort in Nettuno, Italy. Ilya and his family spent two months on the coast of the Tyrrhenian Sea in anticipation of receiving formal paperwork to America. Two families lived in a cottage. There were no windows, only two bedrooms with two bunk beds in each room for a total of eight people. Since there was no dining room, the family ate on a picnic table in the common backyard. It was longest two months of Ilya's life; he even had to sell toy frogs on the beach just to make extra money for the family.

In Russia, Ilya and his family were classified as Jews. Their passports stated their race as "Jewish." During Soviet times, citizens could not openly practice their religion. Vadim wanted to study Physics in a Russian university but was denied a seat, as they had already filled the quota for Jewish students. So, Vadim and Diana both studied computer programming and came to America. In America they were looked at as Anglo or Eastern European Americans, and not as Jews.

Initially, Ilya struggled in school and was not accepted by his peers. He was the new kid in fifth grade and was ridiculed for his accent. He engaged in fights, was not invited to birthday parties, and was emotionally distressed. Israeli children in his apartment complex would also tease him for being Russian and not being a "real Jew." In the sixth grade, things turned around for Ilya. It was middle school, where new students integrated from nearby elementary schools. For the first time in his life, Ilya made American friends.

Vadim's best friends also started to move from Russia, and Ilya suddenly had his own entourage. He was able to socialize with Russian children his age. He translated for them in school and helped them assimilate.

Ilya later reconnected with many of his childhood friends from Russia on the Russian version of classmates.com.

How could he ever forget Polina? Ilya sat next to Polina from first grade through third grade. They were the only two Jewish kids in class, and, as Ilya saw it, forced to sit next to each other, but they became quite good friends. In fact, one day after school they were playing in front of her house, and Ilya won the game and his prize, a kiss. It was Ilya's first kiss. But, to his dismay, Polina's father witnessed this child play and came running after Ilya. Poor Ilya got a beating from her father that night. But, according to him, it was all worth it.

There was also Max. Max was Ilya's best friend and they used to play together after school. One day, the boys tried to cook breakfast (or literally translated, a peasant's omelet) for their mothers. They attempted to cut potatoes, tomatoes, and sausage.

They saw their mothers cooking this breakfast every Sunday, but never knew the order of preparation. In the end, there was a huge mess and no breakfast, but it was a good learning experience. Ironically, Ilya made amazing breakfasts for Asha.

Ilya learned how to swim in the Baltic Sea. As a child, he would sit on the bicycle with his father and ride to the sea. Soviet bicycles have special seats for children in the front of the bicycle. His family owned a summerhouse that was built by his grandfather, and every summer the entire family would stay in that house.

His grandfather was a handyman and could build anything. He worked in a leather factory and his grandmother was the manager. Ilya had so many fond memories of their summerhouse. It was a place where he could play with his cousins freely; where they could pick blackberries, red currant, and gooseberries, make jam, catch fish, and go swimming every day. Ilya loved the water, as did Asha, and he couldn't wait to show Asha his childhood places.

In preparation for their trip, Asha took a Russian class. She was able to learn the Cyrillic alphabet, and even read Russian, but she didn't understand its context. Asha was gifted in the practical arts, and could speak five languages, but Russian for some reason did not come naturally.

Having researched Dementia, she made a conscience effort to develop both sides of her brain. They say Albert Einstein only used ten percent of his brain, can you imagine what he would have accomplished if he had developed both lobes. For that reason, it is important for children to be well-rounded. Asha often wondered how they would raise their kids one day. Would they speak Bengali or Russian? Or both? In many HinJew homes, one culture dominates, but in Asha and Ilya's they worked hard to have a balance.

It was Asha's first trip to Eastern Europe. She was pleasantly surprised. In the first week, they were to meet Ilya's mother's side of the family, and the second week they planned to visit Karlovy Vary and Prague in the Czech Republic.

St. Petersburg is a Tsar's city with palaces and beautifully etched gardens. Ilya's family lived on the outskirts of St.

Petersburg. It felt like an upscale bed and breakfast. Flowers from the family's garden greeted Asha at the airport. They stayed with Ilya's mother's best friend, since Ilya's aunt's husband was an alcoholic. Alcoholism is prevalent among Russian men. It is very common to drink hard alcohol every day. Asha did not drink and was vegetarian, so Ilya's family worried about what she would eat. In fact, their welcome dinner was completely vegetarian! Asha felt right at home. Even though most spoke in Russian, language was not a barrier. Ilya's translation along with lots of body language helped Asha mingle.

The first day, they drove to the summerhouse on the sea. Ilya's grandfather had built the summerhouse and sold it for five thousand U.S. dollars when he left for America. His grandfather had since passed away, but Ilya wanted to share his childhood memories with Asha. So, they decided to pay a visit. After a few detours, they were able to find the street of the summerhouse.

It was the only house on the street that had a balcony; however it was covered in vines, and unrecognizable. The front gate was in chains, but the front door seemed to be cracked open. The silence of the house was unnerving. Ilya's family yelled, "Is anybody home?" Children were playing across the street and the neighbors across the street were watering their plants. "Excuse me; do you know how we can contact the owner of this home? My grandfather . . ." asked Ilya. And before the neighbor could answer, an elderly man was at the gate:

"Can I help you?" he asked in Russian.

Ilya repeated himself, "My grandfather built this house. Do you think we can take a look?" he asked politely.

"Have you come back for the land?" the gentleman grinned.

Ilya explained he wanted to show his wife the house, that's all. The new owner was a seventy-year-old Ukrainian man, tall and morose. It was two o'clock in the afternoon, and Asha could smell alcohol on his breath.

He asked Ilya to follow him, "This used to be the garage, but is now our living room," the tour started. The kitchen was remodeled and decorated with large animals heads from the

Ukrainian's hunting days. The bedrooms were the same, and the backyard was covered in grass, no longer blackberry and red currant bushes. Ilya and his cousins used to play in the creek and explore in the woods. Ilya took videos of everything so he could show his parents. As a child he would ride his bike to the sea. From the summerhouse, it was a ten-minute bike ride.

It was a private beach, visited by locals only. Ilya had taught himself how to swim, as the water was very shallow. It was the Neva River, which flowed to the Baltic Sea and the Gulf of Finland. Asha wanted to swim, but the water was fifteen degrees Celsius in July (even though the air was warm) so she could barely dip her feet in. Ilya, on the other hand, jumped in with his aunt, he was a child once again.

The next stop was the old town. Asha enjoyed its layers of history. It was a modern city built on swampy land. The long summer days with only two hours of dark nights offered plenty of time for sightseeing. It was like any large European city, Asha even found an Indian restaurant. Ilya's family was so interested in Asha's culture. They wanted to wear saris and taste Indian food. In the middle of the old city, they sipped on mango lassi (Indian yogurt drink) and bought Indian spices. Asha promised to show them how to use the spices, and it was agreed that she would cook for the family on the last day.

The castles were extraordinary. Many were gifts from the Tsar and one was for the Empress' lover. She had even built a castle for her lover in Latvia so that he would be comfortable in hiding. The castles had secret passages and were romantic places for Ilya and Asha to explore. The roses were in full bloom and the gardens remarkable. They were superbly planned, with lots of variety.

Asha felt even closer to Ilya after visiting Russia and his family. They treated her just as her family had treated him in India. When everyone gets along, you do not see the differences in a HinJew family.

They continued on to Prague. Before seeing Prague, they took a student agency bus to Karlovy Vary. Karlovy Vary is similar to Calistoga, California, and filled with mineral water and natural hot springs in the mountains. They visited during the International

Film Festival, so travelers from all over the world were in town, including Robert de Niro, Susan Sarandon, etc. They were lucky enough to see a glimpse of them on the red carpet. Booths were set up, and in the hustle and bustle of it all they were able to get a couples' massage to relax.

Prague is a walking city. Asha and Ilya loved to walk and explore the city. Ilya loved the beer; they say Prague offers one of the best beer selections in Europe. Asha worried he would get a beer belly, but he pointed out, "It's not a belly from beer, but a belly for beer!" In all fairness, Ilya also sought out a Vegan restaurant for Asha as most Eastern European cuisine included meat. Prague was flocked by tourists. Its bridges and rivers were on proud display. They went to the Museum of Communism, to a Salvatore Dali exhibit, and to Prague Castle on the top of the Mountain. One cannot sit still in Prague, there is so much to see.

As in India, it would rain heavily for five minutes and then clear up. It was surprisingly humid as well. Jewish Prague was also intact. For some reason, Hitler left Prague's synagogue intact to show people how Jews lived. Asha and Ilya toured the Jewish quarters and indeed visited the Old–New synagogue in Prague, built in the 13th century. It was magical and gave a glimpse into the past. In fact, it is not only the oldest synagogue in Europe (that still operates as a synagogue), but one of the oldest in the world.

They enjoyed Czech cuisine. Asha ate potato dumplings and Ilya tasted the game, but they also loved its Latin food. One night, after dancing in an Argentinean restaurant in the new town, they ran into a Hasidic Jew on the street. Ilya said, "Shalom," and the man responded in very fast Hebrew. "English, English," continued Ilya. "Ah, English, okay, go upstairs," he stated abruptly and started to walk away. Asha and Ilya saw an office building and at 10:00 p.m. didn't think there would be a service in session. "Please, please, go upstairs," the man insisted. "Is there a synagogue here?" Ilya asked, as the man walked away.

Asha and Ilya decided to have a look. There was a prayer room with three Hasidic Jews reading from the Torah, "Welcome," said the one man who spoke English. "Our Rabbi has sent us from Israel for two years, please join us." There were tables for women and men separately and another room for couples to sit together. There were rows and rows of beautiful leather-bound holy books.

One of the men brought Asha and Ilya tea and biscuits. He was shy and did not speak English, but was very sweet and hospitable. They gave them a compact disk of prayers from their Rabbi and asked them to feel at home. One could check their email and pray in the same room, very high-tech. The place was on a main street, but not advertised. Many locals came for Shabbat dinners and services. Asha had seen more extreme Hasidic groups in Jerusalem, and they were both pleasantly surprised to have insight into their world and the internationalism of Judaism.

Asha learned so much about the Jewish culture from this single encounter. They were spiritual, yet modern people. Some practices were similar to those of Hindu people—offering of food, and separating the men and women in the prayer room—Asha was pleased once again to build on their HinJew principles.

~5~

Foray Back to Texas

A month after their visit to Russia, Asha went on a business trip to Dallas, Texas. She was asked to present on behalf of their cancer center by her boss. Although it was a great honor, Asha had not visited Texas since she was born and had mixed feelings. On the other hand, it would be great exposure for her career.

She checked into the hotel and attended a full day of meetings. At night Asha explored downtown Dallas. It was a vibrant city, with nice restaurants and nightlife. She suddenly remembered that Nina's parent's owned a French Restaurant named Quatre Saisons. Jaya had updated Asha on Nina from time to time and she always felt close to her through her mother. Jaya and Sarah had a tradition of exchanging photos of their children during Christmas.

Asha decided to find the restaurant. She searched the Internet and asked the hotel, but there was no restaurant by this name. Asha was determined to find Nina. Asha had left Texas at the age of three and Nina was the only friend she had growing up. So she went to Bijoux, another French Restaurant, and asked about Quatre Saisons.

"Ah, oui oui, Quatre Saisons has become the French Room."

Asha wandered the streets and bumped into a group of white male teenagers who sneered at her:

"Ugh, foreigner . . . , they laughed at her.

"Excuse me; I was born in Texas, you ignorant . . . Asha was furious. Ignorance and arrogance were the two traits she disliked most in people. She had never experienced such racism, but she was not surprised. Asha was excited to find Nina's family, so she "turned the other cheek" and let it go. That became Asha's mantra in life: face it, deal with it, and let it go.

Asha quickly crossed the street, and found the French Room. It was a quaint place and the decor was lovely. Nina was actually half Persian, from her father Farshad, and half Caucasian, by her mother Sarah. It's the Persian culture that has some French influence, so the family went into the restaurant business. Sarah spoke fluent Farsi and blended in nicely with Farshad's family.

"Masha'Allah, Asha is that you?" asked Sarah. "Tell me, how have you been?" Are you married? How are your parents?" she continued. "Narges, dear, can you bring us some tea and pastries?" she instructed the waitress.

"Yes, we are all settled in the San Francisco Bay Area. I am married and work in cancer research. My parents are retired and enjoying being grandparents."

"Do you have children? How many?" Sarah asked.

"No, but my brother had a son. My nephew is adorable. By the way, how is Nina?"

Sarah looked away, "Nina married a deejay and we don't see much of her nowadays," she said in disappointment. "We used to talk on the phone every day, but that has changed," she added.

"Do you know how I can find her? I would love to see her," asked Asha.

"Well, she works at the Central Market, maybe you can find her there."

The next morning, Asha was to fly home, but on the way to the airport she stopped by the Central Market. It was an earthy store with fresh organic produce and meats, and luckily Nina was working that day. Asha had very little time and waited in anticipation. After nearly fifteen minutes, a brunette lady was walking toward her.

Wait, that can't be her, she's a blonde! They were salt and pepper. Nina was born a blonde, but the Persian traits dominated and her hair became much darker.

"Nina, is that you? Do you remember me?" asked Asha.

"Yes, of course I do, it's been thirty years!" said Nina.

"Can you take a coffee break, I have a few minutes before I catch a flight?" asked Asha.

"Sure, yeah, have a seat (still in amazement that Asha is standing in front of her) how is everything with you?" said Nina.

"Good, I'm married and live in California," she said. "Is he Indian?" Nina asked.

"No he's a Russian Jew, can you believe it?" "Wow, that's great, sounds interesting," said Nina.

"How about you? How have you been? I stopped by the restaurant and they said . . ."

"Yes, I know, my parents don't approve of my husband," explained Nina.

"I know the feeling; my parents asked that I not marry a Muslim or a Christian, which make up half of the world's population! Deep inside, I knew whoever I chose would be okay; he just happened to be Jewish. Anyway, tell me about your husband. Is he a nice person? Does he treat you right?" asked Asha.

"Well . . . he is a nice person, but, recently, he's been stealing my money to purchase marijuana. He's even made purchases on my credit card." She took a deep breath and continued, "I can't get him to stop; he has become addicted, and lost his ambition for life. He loves his music and that's all he needs," she said in frustration.

"Well, does he want help? It can take time, but eventually he'll grow out of it," said Asha.

"I hope so; I want to start a family. How about you? Are you trying?" asked Nina.

"Every day!" exclaimed Asha.

"Listen (as Asha glanced at her watch and felt disappointed that she had to end the conversation), I have to catch a flight, but can we continue this over the phone?" Asha continued.

"Sure, give me a call anytime," said Nina. They exchanged information.

People enter your lives for a reason. Asha felt she was meant to reconnect with Nina and help her in some way. Throughout the flight, Asha was wondering how she could help Nina's husband stop this behavior. Behavior change can take years, and the person has to be willing to change.

How could she marry someone who stole from her? How can you have a relationship if there is no trust? Asha was upset that Nina would allow someone to take advantage of her in this way. She even ignores her own family to support his bad habits; there must be a healthier solution.

Asha looked into resources at the hospital and did some research. She was able to find some health care centers close to Nina so they could try therapy. Asha called Nina, but there was no answer. Was it the wrong number? Did Nina not want her help? Would she ever hear from her again? The next day, Asha called the Central Market and left a message for Nina.

Months went by, and Asha never heard from Nina. Nina was innocent and Asha wanted to help her. After all the years of community service, and volunteering at women's shelters, the least she could do was help a friend; a friend who didn't seem to want her help. There was an evil force that was pulling Nina's husband. It happens to all of us. Sometimes the evil force is stronger than the good; this is when you lose balance. And it's okay to lose balance from time to time, but if the evil is too strong, you risk losing everything. Asha wanted to pull Nina away, but she never returned her calls.

Asha thought of Nina often. She wanted to introduce her to Ilya. She wanted Ilya to meet a nice Persian family. Asha had many close Middle-Eastern friends, but every time they were discussed, the conversations somehow shifted to Israel. Israel was a touchy subject.

Ilya and his family had close ties to Israel. But Asha always felt like there were two sides to every story. She had visited Israel and studied its history to better understand Ilya and his family. But she could not deny the stories of the Palestinian people. Asha had a co-worker, Mo, who was born in Jerusalem. His family is Christian and lives in the West Bank. But since he holds a

Palestinian ID card, he cannot fly directly into Israel to see his family. He must fly into Jordan and cross multiple security checkpoints in order to visit his family. It seems like a lot of hurdles just to see the family. Both countries want peace, but bureaucracy stands in the way.

Similar ethnic hatred exists between India and Pakistan. And these two HinJew countries—India and Israel—are fighting against the same enemy. Israel is like a pond of fishes surrounded by alligators. India borders Pakistan, which houses terrorists. In 1992, the Indo-Israeli defense agreement was established as a counterterrorism strategy and to form a military relationship between India and Israel. In fact, Israel supplies arms to India, and one would think that the two countries would become allies one day. But discussions between Ilya and Asha got heated so they often avoided the topic.

In fact, there were several topics that they differed on. It was hard for Asha to understand Ilya at times. His family spoke in Russian and she often felt left out. Ilya was a daunting husband and always translated for her, but it could be very difficult to feel included when those around you speak another tongue. So Asha had made friends with Ilya's niece, Lea, who loved to speak in English. Lea could speak Russian and English at the age of three.

Like Lea, Asha was always mature for her age and related to those older than she. She was the eldest of two children and had always wanted an older sibling. She admired professors and respected those who were intelligent. It is for this reason she pursued a career in academia. She had friends with similar degrees who worked in industry and had their own companies, and although she respected her friends, she always believed in balance. She had considered being an entrepreneur so she would be able to work for herself, but she didn't want to work 80 hours a week.

"Maybe you could open a Laundromat, there are small overhead costs and you don't have to hire staff," a friend once suggested. Asha researched franchises, thought of getting additional licenses, but in the end was content with her career. She was home by 5:00 p.m. and could have dinner with her husband by 7:00 p.m.

Marriage was a different story. Although Asha loved Ilya, it was difficult at times. Love doesn't pay one's bills. A part of her felt like she failed her parents by not marrying an Indian doctor. Another part of her felt that maybe Ilya's family really wanted him to marry a Jewish girl.

Asha began to develop insecurities about being the first HinJew couple in both families. But did she really want to spend the rest of her life trying to gain his family's approval? No, not really. Did Ilya have pressure to carry on the family name and Jewish traditions? Of course he did. Initially, they did the weekly Shabbat dinners, and monthly family birthday celebrations, but it was too much. Asha felt suffocated and questioned if marriage was really for her.

Trust was also an issue. When Ilya and Asha dated, Ilya was thinking about applying to graduate school. Asha had a Master's degree and was familiar with the application process. She spent nearly a year preparing for Ilya's application only to find out that he had lied to her about his grades. It was not a miscalculation from quarter to semester units. It was a lie. He lied about his grades to impress Asha and unfortunately she did not check his transcripts until he was ready to submit the application. This was the first lie in what would turn out to be a series of lies.

Ilya deliberately gave Asha the wrong information, whether it was about how many drinks he had at happy hour, or whether he smoked cigarettes at a party with his friends. In Russian culture, drinking and smoking at a party would not be an issue. But, Jaya and Akash did not smoke or drink, and to Asha this was an issue. Ilya lied to Asha because he knew she did not like drinking or smoking. To her, without trust you have nothing. But she also realized she was trying to control his Russian behavior.

Asha knew Ilya loved her dearly, but, due to the lies, she doubted him. It was not a good feeling, and she took measures to protect her and her family's assets. She did not want to spend the rest of her life as a private investigator. Instead, she and Ilya sought sessions with a marriage counselor and hoped they were on the path of healing. Marriage is hard work. Marriage is sacrifice. There is no recipe book for it. But Asha and Ilya grew together and finally started to understand the roles and responsibilities of marriage. Luckily, they adjusted in the first two years, as many couples do.

"You know, I'd like to buy something for the house. But, it seems you have everything you need," said Ilya. Ilya had moved into Asha's house when they married and he felt like he wanted to contribute.

"It's okay; we will need to replace things eventually."

"What about a new TV?"

"I rarely watch TV, but, sure, if you want to."

"Great, but we'll first need to drill holes in the wall, install an access panel for the wires, and then mount it," continued Ilya.

Ilya was excited about the TV. It was their first home improvement project they did together after he moved into her house. The second was their garden of herbs and spices. That is how you build a home. Buying furniture together and deciding which family to spend holidays with, those are the types of arguments she still looked forward to. Asha appreciated that Ilya cared so much for the TV and kept it clean. She had never watched so many movies in her life, but it was something they did together, so she also enjoyed it. Sometimes, something as simple as buying a TV can remind you of that.

In fact, Asha would always think in terms of "we" or "us" and was very loyal, maybe to a fault. After marriage, she gave up some of her closest friends out of respect for her husband. She was very sensitive to his feelings, so much that she started to neglect herself and her friends. It was not healthy. She used to be a very social person and loved to entertain guests. So she did not understand this change. Her husband came back from work and went to the gym, while she came back from work and started to cook dinner. Occasionally, she would meet her girlfriends for lunch or coffee, but it was a rarity. She wanted to stay home and build her nest, while her husband wanted to go to the next Russian party.

Is marriage supposed to feel like you are living in a cage? Maybe it is a cage. It was exhausting at times, and she didn't know if she was the only one invested in the marriage. She remembered their priests' blessings, "May your home be a shelter against the storms of life, a haven of harmony, balance, and peace, a stronghold of faith in your destiny together, and a place of love and compassion." She often focused on the similarities between the two cultures in order to make it work. During these low points, Asha and Ilya often referred back to their Ketubah:

"We pledge to support, provide for, cherish, and honor each other in faith; to strive always to be sensitive to each other's needs; to recognize and respect our differences and to nurture each other's growth, so that we can attain mutual, intellectual, emotional, physical, and spiritual fulfillment, we shall work together to reach an openness which will enable us to share with each other our thoughts, feelings, and experience, through life's joy and sorrow."

By re-reading the Ketubah, Asha and Ilya were back on track. Asha lit a little fire under Ilya, and he stepped up his duties as a husband. Together, they constructed a plan for each month: two weekends would be devoted to themselves, one weekend to family, and one weekend to friends.

~6~

Karma

Finances can make or break a couple. Asha came from a wealthy family, and she never really needed money. For that reason, she didn't want it to be an issue. There were times when Ilya seemed more like a roommate than a husband.

Ilya and Asha shared the monthly costs and performed a duet of household chores. He put the clothes into the laundry machine. She folded. He chopped the vegetables. She cooked. He washed the dishes. She emptied. He planted the seeds into pots. She watered. Although this helped to create a bond, Asha never stopped feeling like a private investigator. Ilya would often come to bed late, and if they had a disagreement, he would go for a walk and disappear for an hour. It was this continued behavior that was a real concern for Asha. Was she too controlling? Was she becoming paranoid since Ilya had lied to her so many times before?

One day, Asha received a call from the ER. "Mrs. Zalan, your husband is in the ER," said the nurse, "he wanted to call and let you know, but he's on morphine and unable to speak at the moment. Are you able to come pick him up?" "Of course, I'm on my way," said Asha. It was 11:30 a.m., close to the lunch hour. Asha dropped everything at work and rushed to the hospital.

Ilya's shoulder was dislocated and blood was seeping through the bandages all over his leg. "Are you okay? What happened?" asked Asha.

"I'm so happy you came to the ER, can you take me home?" Ilya was still medicated. He had fallen down some stairs on his way to the Metro.

"I was in the city, so I decided to visit my old co-workers," explained Ilya.

"No problem, I'm glad you came to the ER, I will take you home," said Asha. "Are you feeling better? I was so scared when they called me at work. Sorry, it took me so long to get here."

"No, I'm sorry," confessed Ilya.

"What do you mean? It was an accident."

"I'll explain in the car," he insisted.

During their dating phase, Asha and Ilya had taken a break. It was during this break that Ilya had been intimate with his ex-coworker Maya. Maya was attractive and Jewish. Everybody has a past, so it was a non-issue until Maya resurfaced.

"I was in the city, and ran into Maya," continued Ilya. "Nothing happened, she just walked me to the Metro, and that's it."

Asha was silent. There were so many thoughts racing through her head. She wanted to trust him, and knew that he was telling the truth, but why did she feel so hurt? She became aggressive, and started yelling at Ilya, "What, you met with Maya behind my back? Why didn't you tell me about it? Is there anything else I need to know?" she asked.

"No, that's it. I spoke to my old boss and ran into her, it was not planned, I promise," he said. Ilya denied everything, so Asha had to trust him.

Women are innately jealous creatures. But Asha was a realist. She was assertive and always presented the facts. It's when you overanalyze the facts that you start to doubt the truth. Asha decided to be content with the fact that he told her what happened and left it at that. After all, if Ilya did something wrong, then he earned his punishment of a dislocated shoulder.

Behavior change cannot happen if the person does not accept that s/he has a problem. Ilya would often play the victim and proclaim, "I didn't do anything wrong" or shift the blame to Asha. He used every tactic possible to not take ownership for his actions. Even the marriage counselor suggested Ilya get counseling for himself, but he refused. He admitted to his lies to Asha because he knew the guilt would eat him up on the inside. So why did he continue to lie? It was a bad habit. Asha felt helpless at times, and tried to move forward. She married the man, so had to give it her best effort.

Asha often wondered if she married an Indian man, would he understand her better. If you come from the same culture, do you share the same values? Not necessarily. Asha's parents came to the U.S. more than thirty years ago and still hold on to the values they learned thirty years ago. Today, India is a very different country due to globalization. It is new money and people are losing the qualities that are "Indian." Asha observed the women who immigrate from India today and her cousins living in India, and they are much savvier than she ever was at their age.

Asha learned Hindi by watching Hindi movies. She was lucky to meet and take pictures with quite a few Bollywood (India's Hollywood) actors and she cherished these encounters. She often wore kurtis (Indian tops) to work and traditional Indian outfits to parties. Indian women would often smirk at her as they walked by in their trendy skirts and boots. She could never forget the vivid images from the clubs she went to in India. She remembered going into a bathroom of a nightclub in Bombay when she was twenty-one years old. There were young girls inside the bathroom in miniskirts.

"What are you wearing? Aren't you cold?" asked Asha.

"No."

"Are you doing drugs in the sink?" she confronted the girls.

The girls just laughed at her, "You Americans feel so entitled. India will surpass you in five years, just watch," they laughed.

"How old are you anyway?" Asha continued in an attempt to combat this problem, but the girls walked away.

Asha was disgusted. She saw firsthand the effects of modernization on these girls. But, drugs are drugs, and she was very disappointed. It was as if she was watching her sisters do this and wanted to offer them help. Westernization is more than sex, drugs, and rock and roll, as they say. When Asha saw a problem, she wanted to fix it. But, in the end she realized that Indians raised in the U.S. are much more "Indian" than the ones raised in India, and there was nothing she could to about it. India was moving at a fast pace.

Many of Asha's cousins in India wanted to study in the U.S. At some point they became engineers and worked for U.S. companies. Some of her cousins pursued Ph.D.s or MBAs and competed with thousands of students for a seat in a university. Some cousins found their mates online, married them, and moved to the U.S. Others were content in India, as their families were wealthy and they had comfortable lives so they had no desire to come to the U.S. They realized that in the U.S. not everyone can afford personal cleaners, cooks, and drivers. Did they really want to wash their own dishes? Or buy their own groceries?

Everything is available in India, from the latest electronics to luxury cars. In fact, India's economy ranks in the top-ten wealthiest economies in the world. It is worth more than $2 trillion dollars. The problem is that it belongs to a small percentage of the total population.

The opposite holds true for Russia. Ilya's family in Russia is upper middle class, but cannot live the life as his family does in the U.S. Russia's cost of living, especially in urban cities, has become too costly. New money can barely buy one a decent life. Vadim's family all lived in the U.S. comfortably, but Diana's family lived in Russia. Diana would send money to her sister every month to help with their finances.

Similar expectations were imposed on Asha's family. Akash and Jaya were happy to help family members in need. They financed their nephews' and nieces' education and paid for home repairs in Akash's parents' home. It was like a steady cash flow to their parents through the umbilical cord. In India, it is the eldest son's duty to care for his parents. That changed in Asha's family, when Arun escaped his duties by moving to the East Coast. He left for a higher-paying job. But is there really that much difference between a two million dollar home in Washington D.C., and a five million dollar home in the San Francisco Bay Area? There is no limit to material wealth.

If money is acquired for need, it's okay because there is an end. But, when money is a want, there can be no end. Asha lived within her means, while Arun always wanted more. As the Jewish saying goes: If you can fix your problem with money, then it's not a problem, it's an expense. What is wealth, if you cannot help someone in need like your parents? Asha planned to take care of her parents in their old age.

Asha was Askash and Jaya's power of attorney. When Jaya had an emergent case of appendicitis, it was Asha who was by her side. At the age of sixty, it is rare to have appendicitis, but Jaya was lucky. When Jaya had a rotator cuff surgery, it was Asha who signed the discharge papers in the hospital and made sure she performed the physical therapy exercises. When Akash and Jaya were held back in India due to airplane strikes, it was Asha who overnighted them an additional one-month supply of their medications.

Akash and Jaya had filed their advance directives with their physician, but Asha would be the one to carry out their orders. A living will was also in place, so there would be no sibling rivalry. Akash made it clear that he wanted his ashes to return to India and be poured into the Ganges, India's holy river. Jaya on the other hand did not want to be resuscitated if she ever became non-responsive. Nor did she want life support. She was also okay with local arrangements, and had no desire for her ashes to return to India. Asha would protect their wishes since they had done so much for her. She figured one day she might need help too.

It is the principle of cause and effect or as it's known in Hindu culture, Karma. Hindus believe in the transformation of the soul. Asha believed if she performed good deeds for others (good karma), she would find peace. Generally, there are four types of karma: *Sanchita* (total), *Praarabdha* (fruitful or problems in the present life), *Kriyamana* (instant or what is produced in the current life), and *Aagami* (future). The chain of actions will effect lifetimes to come.

~7~

A Little Miracle

Getting pregnant is one-third the woman, one-third the man, and one-third the unknown. It's hard to say exactly what combination results in pregnancy. Ilya and Asha made a pact to never blame each other. If it was meant to be, it would happen for them. In the meantime their nieces and nephews kept them busy. In total, they had five nieces and nephews, and more than twenty cousins. It took a lot of time and energy to keep in touch with these family members, in addition to friends. Children are precious, and Ilya and Asha loved them.

"Okay, we'll be back by nine o'clock. She knows how to brush her teeth, all you need to do is put on her pajamas, and read her a story, and she will go to sleep," instructed Elena.

"Sounds good, have fun at the concert," said Ilya.

"Okay, bye. Call us if you need anything" said Elena. "We're just a ten-minute drive away, so don't hesitate to call," she reiterated.

"Don't worry, have a good time; we'll take care of the rest."

Asha was on her cell phone and Ilya was holding his niece Lea. As soon as her parents walked out the door, she started to cry. So Ilya ran for toys and Asha ran for food in the refrigerator. Asha looked frantically for string cheese or chocolate. Lea's cries stopped abruptly; there was pin-drop silence, and then a loud sound.

In a blink of an eye, Lea had pushed the screen off their second floor window and had fallen through it. She was waving bye-bye to her parents and next thing you know, she had plummeted to the ground. Blood was profuse and Lea's head had cracked open.

Asha could hear Elena screaming outside, "No, no, my babychka . . . it's okay baby, it's okay . . . Ilya call 911 now!" she yelled in despair, still hazy in tears. Ilya called the police, and Asha ran down the stairs to help Elena with Lea. The ambulance screeched its way into the driveway and Lea was transported to a nearby children's trauma hospital.

Lea was in a coma. Asha and Ilya felt so responsible and visited Lea every day. They sang her favorite songs to her, while holding her hand. Asha debated with herself if she could feel life in her hand, but she knew that Lea could hear them.

At night, when the parents were at the hospital, Vadim and Diana took care of Lea's brother. He was too young to understand what was going on with his sister. He instead enjoyed his time playing with his grandparents.

Lea was four years old and had her entire life ahead of her. How could this happen to a child? It was not fair. Why do bad things happen to good people? Weeks went by, and there were no signs of her awakening. All they could do was pray, pray to all the Gods. After all, the power of prayer can have healing effects on the human body.

This was God's test. Asha's family had experienced a similar test when her mother's younger sister, Lily, was diagnosed with fourth stage adenocarcinoma (liver cancer). In this fourth stage of cancer, it had metastasized and spread to other organs throughout her body. Asha was in London when Lily was diagnosed. The family spared her the news until her arrival. Lily had greeted Asha at the airport with deep, yellow, jaundiced eyes. Asha knew something was wrong, but it did not make sense. She was a vegetarian, a nonsmoker, never consumed alcohol, cared for children as a nanny, and was a kind person. There was no family history of cancer and the doctors could not find its origin. Akash and Jaya brought her to America and did everything they could to provide her the best treatment possible. She was a transplant candidate, but too weak for the operation. Asha tried to make her life comfortable. She placed a rocking chair in her room, played her favorite music, and massaged her every day.

Lily had gone through a divorce. In India, during her time, divorce was a sin. But, it was not her choice. Later it was known that the only reason her husband married her was because he knew Lily's sister lived in the U.S. and he wanted to practice medicine abroad. Jaya had started the paperwork to move to America, but it can take years for sponsorship. Lily's husband grew skeptical and left her. They were married for less than a year. Asha felt that her aunt had internalized these emotions, which literally devoured her organs.

Emotions and social relationships can have a physiological effect on the human body, known as the psychosomatic response. Lily passed away at the age of forty-nine. Jaya cried for years as she went through the rituals of death and morning. Asha felt like she had lost a second mother. She dedicated her life to cancer research and worked in the same university where her aunt had been treated. It was a very painful time for the family, as was this time with Lea's illness.

Ilya experienced every emotion possible, from anger to guilt. He was not a very emotional person like Asha, and normally positive and calm under pressure. But he had nightmares at night, and could not sleep for months. He felt emptiness inside him, and developed irritable bowel syndrome. He could not forgive himself for what had happened. And how could his sister or brother-in-law David ever forgive him? He was not a religious person, but he and Asha prayed for Lea together every night before they went to sleep. Elena and David were role models for them, and although Ilya and Asha did not have children of their own, they felt as if they had lost a child.

Life is precious. Asha learned so much through Lea. She learned how delicate life can be. She decided to erase the slate and forgive Ilya for all his wrongdoings. After all, we are human beings and people make mistakes. She could still see love in his eyes and knew that he had a heart of gold. So she reprogrammed her mind and deleted all her anger toward him.

It was killing her inside to see him so depressed. She wanted to start over and somehow felt much closer to him. She thought to herself, what if I lost Ilya? "Think happy thoughts, think happy thoughts," she repeated in her head. Why was this happening to their family? Asha had been through so many tests in her life previously, and now they were experiencing one as a couple.

"Mama," said Lea. Lea's vital signs were normal. She was lucky and had very little brain damage. Pilot holes were drilled and her skull did open, but the neurosurgeons were able to join it back together. Post-surgery she had to wear a helmet to sleep at night. Asha's good friend from college was a pediatric neurologist and able to refer the family to a well-known specialist. Lea was on the path to recovery.

Lea was given a second chance at life. Elena reassured Asha and Ilya that it was not their fault. Asha took her to physical therapy appointments and noticed improvements in her activities of daily living.

Ilya stepped up and took on his role as an uncle. He woke up one morning and realized what his role would be in Lea's life. He wanted to attend her ballet performances, to cook for her, and to take her to movies. He wanted to swim with her and teach her new tricks. Before the accident, Lea was very musical and loved to dance. But she lost some of her motor function and was unable to move to music as she used to. It was a glimpse at parenthood for Asha and Ilya, and they would overcome this challenge together.

~8~

It's a Boy!

Social media is more powerful than war. It can reach millions of people and spread information in seconds. One day a seventeen-year-old boy named Santiago messaged Ilya via Facebook. He ignored the messages, but noticed they became more frequent. Ilya did not recognize a single person on Santiago's contact list; they were all located in South America. A month later, when he saw Sofia's name in the subject line, he decided to respond:

> Dear Santiago,
>
> Thank you for contacting me. I understand from your messages that you feel I know your mother. It is true that I traveled in Sud America fifteen years ago, and met your mother. It seems like you need my help. Please let me know.
>
> Best,
> Ilya

Santiago responded the very next day.

> Dear Ilya,
>
> According to my mother, you were very close. You two met in Argentina and spent many weeks together. She spoke good

things of you and your conversations. I am coming to look at schools in San Francisco and hope we can meet soon.

Respectfully,
Santiago

Ilya agreed to meet Santiago. He was curious. Did Sofia want to tell him something? Ilya wondered about Sofia from time to time, but did not keep in touch with her out of respect for Asha. Surprisingly, Asha was okay with the meeting with Santiago. Maybe Santiago wanted a mentor for his studies? Maybe he was networking and looking for jobs? Ilya did not want to spend the next few weeks guessing. He had been through enough with Lea and was still down on life. He couldn't handle any more surprises at the moment. He decided to message Santiago once more before his visit.

Dear Santiago,

Please let me know when you arrive in San Francisco and we can meet in a restaurant. You can call me at (415) 757-6070.

Thank you,
Ilya

Santiago's mother had been killed in a car accident six weeks before and he had not yet had time to grieve his mother's death properly. In addition, he had to pack her belongings and manage her property. He needed help and felt that it was time to meet his father. Ilya was Santiago's biological father.

Sofia lived with men periodically, but Santiago never felt a connection to them, and felt incomplete. He always wondered about the roots of his family and prayed that he would have the opportunity to meet his father one day. But how would he know him? Or did a part of him already know? Santiago had seen photos of Ilya and he looked very much like him: tall, dark hair, and medium build. He was nervous, but hoped that his father would take him in and that they would be able to start a relationship.

His entire life he had dreamt of how it would feel to live as a nuclear family. He knew from his mother's face how much Ilya meant to her, but he never understood why they could not speak or see each other. He imagined the conversations he would have with his father and was excited that this day had come. He had waited seventeen years.

Would his mother's death bring them closer together? Would Ilya want to have a relationship with his son? What if his father already had other children, would he be willing to have more? Santiago had so many questions for his father. He had always yearned for his love and affection. In fact, there were only women and aunties in his life, and he lacked a male role model. On a positive note, he knew everything about women, their likes and dislikes, and could make a woman very happy one day.

He was focused on his studies and career. He wanted to be an engineer and help develop products that were better for the environment. He did not have any expectations, but was open to studying in the U.S. if it meant he would be closer to his father. He felt that his life was about to change forever.

"Hola, Santiago, bienvenidos a California," greeted his uncle Jaime. "How was the flight? Did they feed you? Your aunt Lucia is very excited to meet you and is waiting for you at home. We are all very sorry to hear about your mother. We loved her so much." Jaime was so excited to see his nephew that Santiago did not have time to respond.

Santiago had butterflies in his stomach. He had only met his uncle once as a child, but had spoken to him on the phone many times. He held on to his hug and did not want to let go. Jaime was close to his sister and promised Sofia that he would take care of his son if anything happened to her. Jaime and Lucia were his new parents, at least for now.

"This is your room. It used to be your cousin's, but he lives in San Diego now. It's so nice to have you here, the house is full again," described Jaime. Jaime and Lucia lived most of their lives in Miami, but left to purchase an avocado farm north of San Diego. Jaime worked out of his Bay Area office, but planned to retire in San Diego.

Santiago settled in nicely. He never had his own room before and used to sleep in his dining room. His aunt and uncle's generosity overwhelmed him. As weeks passed, it started to feel like home. He helped Lucia around the house, something her own children never did. Santiago was well-versed in housework, his mother had taught him well. He kept busy with thinking about school and started to look into universities. But all he could think about since his arrival was his father. It was time to meet him.

Jaime called Ilya and invited him over for lunch. "Ilya, my name is Jaime Llanos, I am Sofia's older brother. Santiago is living with us and he would like to meet you. Are you available this Saturday?" The date was set, and Lucia practiced with Santiago on how he should break the news to Ilya that he had a son.

Ilya did not know if he should go alone or bring Asha. He was nervous and did not know what to expect. He had worked so hard to gain her trust back, so he had to tell her. He spoke to Asha and they agreed to go together on Saturday. Asha was surprisingly calm about it. If this was important to Ilya, then it was important to Asha.

Asha brought flowers and a bottle of Malbec, Ilya's favorite Argentinean wine. They drove to Jaime and Lucia's house. Jaime greeted them at the door and introductions were made among the adults. Santiago made his entrance:

"My name is Santiago, I am your son," Santiago was forthright and did not waste any time.

"Bienvenidos," greeted Ilya. He was focused on remembering his Spanish and the message did not register immediately.

"I have waited my whole life to meet you," said Santiago.

Ilya felt dizzy and fainted. His face turned blue. "Wake up, wake up. Are you okay?" repeated Santiago. Ilya was shocked and did not know what to say. He could not stop staring at his son; he was handsome and fit. Asha comforted Ilya and grinned at Santiago. Could this be true?

Yes, it was true. Sofia and Ilya had a son together and Ilya had no idea. He had just been through so much with Lea's accident and did not know if he could handle this situation. Asha stepped up to the fire, "Santiago, we are delighted to meet you and very sorry to hear about your mother," she assured him. "We are so glad that you contacted us."

Silence took over the room. Lucia and Asha headed to the kitchen. "Can I offer you a drink?" asked Lucia. "I do not drink," said Asha, "but maybe for Ilya." She figured he needed a drink. Ilya walked over to the couch, his legs weak at the knees.

He was so confused and had so many questions for Santiago. But he was at a loss for words. "Sofia was an amazing woman and how could I not be in this boy's life. He probably resents me and must have so much anger toward me," he thought to himself. He doubted himself and was not sure if he was up for the challenge.

Ilya eventually built up the nerve to speak to Santiago, "Well, maybe we can spend some time together next week, how does that sound?" The boy's face lit up. He was ecstatic and felt all his dreams come true. He imagined different versions of the same scenario and it would be etched in his memory for years.

"Lunch is served," called Lucia.

"Let's continue over lunch," said Jaime.

Santiago would be a new addition to their family. Asha and Ilya would have the family they always wanted. Granted, it's not how they planned it, but maybe it could work. Asha had her doubts, but having just been through Lea's accident together, she felt that they were stronger than ever. Maybe it would not be a good fit, but it was worth a try.

From time to time, Asha felt that if she could not have any children of her own, they could adopt or become foster parents. Ilya was open to the idea of adoption, but still wanted to try to have children of his own. Ilya knew that Asha would be a great mother and would give Santiago so much affection. She would often sing to Lea and Lea felt close to Asha. Children could feel her warmth, and Santiago needed to be loved. Although he missed his mother dearly and carried a photo of the two of them in his wallet, he really liked Asha. It felt natural to him. He needed his father, and Asha was willing to take him in for Ilya's sake.

Santiago continued to live with Jaime and Lucia and they often spent time together with Ilya and Asha. Jaime's son would graduate and move back home in six months. It was decided that at that time, Santiago would go live with Ilya and Asha. Ilya was so proud to have a son. He always wanted a son. He was sensitive to Asha's feelings, but she too was fond of Santiago. He seemed like a gift from God and blended in nicely.

Asha, Ilya, and Santiago became a family. Santiago slowly began to heal his wounds and was able to speak openly about Sofia. It was not easy being raised by a single parent. Ilya in many ways felt a sense of responsibility even though he was never told about his son. Santiago had been raised Catholic, but was eager to learn the Hindu and Jewish ways of life. He researched both extensively and they started going to a church with families of multi-religions and cultures. It was the perfect solution and he did not feel alien any longer.

~9~

Los Padres

Santiago was in the top five percent of his class. He loved mathematics and wanted to study engineering. Both Asha and Ilya worked in healthcare and had limited technical skills, but Ilya's parents' were both programmers, so it was part of his genetic makeup. Santiago would do whatever it took to make his father proud.

But assimilation was difficult. He struggled with English and the Mexican students ridiculed his Spanish accent. Spanish accents vary by region, if you are from the mountains, Spain, or Latin America. The Argentine accent where Santiago was from is instantly recognizable throughout the Spanish world. 20th century Buenos Aires novelists preserved this speech as a literary style. The influence of Italian has even led to the development of a separate language, *Lunfardo*, which blends Spanish and Italian. Sofia used to write *Lunfardo* poetry and left many pieces behind for Santiago. It is through her poetry that Santiago was able to understand his mother. Her beauty came across in her words.

Luckily for Santiago, Asha spoke both Spanish and Italian, and was able to understand him. Asha helped Santiago learn English and tutored him three days a week after school. This was their special time together and Santiago grew closer to Asha, she was like a new mother to him. She also taught him Hindu philosophies as well as Jewish principles. "All religions are the same," she taught him.

Santiago had been raised Catholic, but did not believe in God. He was angry with God for taking his father away from him. As far as he was concerned, God was only for people who needed it. During his formative years, he needed a father. Men came and went, and although they were all very nice to him, they were not his father. Santiago spent many years looking for Ilya, but Sofia said he left before Santiago was born and she did not know where he lived. Santiago never knew his father's last name until his mother's death. His father had been dead to him.

The bond between Ilya and Santiago was like the top layer of crème brûlée, delicate and able to break at any time. Ilya had become silent around Santiago. He felt very uncomfortable around his son. There was something that scared him. Ilya often stared at Santiago and said nothing. One day his tongue slipped:

"You have your mother's eyes; I can't stop thinking about her."

"Do you still remember how she looks?" asked Santiago.

"I don't know, I think about her from time to time, but since you have been living with us, I can't stop thinking about her . . . us. I'll never forget the time we spent together," continued Ilya.

"What were you doing in Sud America?" asked Santiago.

"It was a summer vacation, and the only reason I returned to California was to start university."

Teardrops were running down Asha's face, she overheard the tail end of the conversation. She knew Ilya loved her, but was he completely over Sofia? Was he ready to be a father? Ilya was fast approaching forty, and the thought of having children had been on his mind for some time. He definitely wanted children with Asha and maybe this would be good practice.

Asha in fact seemed much closer to Santiago than Ilya. So she decided to take a step back and not get too close to Santiago. She wanted Ilya to take responsibility for his son and to develop a relationship with him. Ilya figured the only way to his son was through sports.

Santiago had played fútbol since he was five years old. He practiced every day after school in the park by his home. Fútbol is indeed the most popular sport in the world. He played for himself; it was his therapy. When he played, he felt free, free from his nightmares about his mother, free from English, and free from his peers who seemed to have a problem with his Spanish accent. He prayed to the soccer field and hoped that Ilya could play with him one day. "Father, do you play fútbol?" he asked eagerly.

"I used to play in high school, maybe we can play some time?" stated Ilya. They started that very Saturday.

Ilya was mesmerized by his skills, his son was fast and Ilya could hardly keep up. They decided to warm up together, but Santiago could not hold back.

"Have you ever thought of playing for the school? It would be a great way to meet others," asked Ilya.

"It's something I do for myself, that's all," said his son. The truth is he didn't want to give the other kids an opportunity to ridicule, but he did play for a team in Argentina.

"Maybe we could check out a game together and then decide?" Ilya persisted. Santiago agreed only to make his father happy. It seemed important to his father, so he would do it.

This is not another story of a high school coach discovering the next Ronaldo or Messi. This was about the father–son bond and the strength of positive reinforcement. Children are eager to gain the praise of their parents. It was fútbol and his new parents that made this transition bearable for Santiago. His bereavement period was shortened due to his relocation. He still had many unresolved feelings inside and was able to channel them through sports.

"Would you like to be my assistant coach?" asked the high school head coach. Santiago was just finishing high school and consumed by college applications. Maybe this could be a bridge for him until he was admitted to a university. "Sure, but only through the summer," agreed Santiago.

"Sounds good, you start on Monday," confirmed the head coach. Santiago was the new assistant coach of his high school soccer team. His responsibilities included assisting the head coach in all aspects of daily operations of the men's soccer program, from recruiting, on-field coaching, travel arrangements, and equipment ordering. He also wanted fútbol to be accessible to all children and implemented a minority recruitment plan.

Not only did he mentor on the field, he also became a mathematics tutor. It was these extracurricular activities that earned him admission into one of the finest schools on the West Coast, Stanford University. But unfortunately he could not afford the tuition, so he started at a junior college near his home, and transferred to a state university. He saved time and money and was able to finish his engineering degree in three years. Ilya and Asha were so proud of his son and supported his decision to pursue his new career in the computer gaming industry. Santiago was headed to Japan.

~10~

Hiragana and Katakana

Japan loved Santiago. He was thrilled about his new job, the language, and the women. He remembered the philosophies Asha taught him and he started living them. The Japanese were so respectful and did everything to perfection. He was highly influenced by his roommates, Kanichiro and Daisaku.

They too were engineers working for U.S. companies in Japan. Kanichiro or Kan for short was his best friend, he was known as "Kan the Man" to Santiago. The three of them became very close. Daisaku or Dai was heavy on the bar scene and in love with Russian girls. He wanted to meet Ilya badly and thought he would introduce him to Russian girls. Kan also liked Western girls. For some reason Kan and Dai did not like Japanese girls, but Santiago loved them.

Santiago took Japanese classes before going to Japan, and he could write in both *Hiragana* and *Katakana*, two Japanese syllabary styles. He also learned to speak Japanese fluently thanks to Kan and Dai. Santiago soon felt the expenses piling up and did not want to burden his father, so he decided to look for a job. He needed a second job to make ends meet in Japan. There were many opportunities to teach English, but his English was not so good.

The only thing that was missing in his life was fútbol. He tried desperately to find an intramural team so he could play on the weekends. But it occurred to him that he could also coach or become a referee. He was able to find the latter position and started to referee intercollegiate fútbol games. The Japanese players liked him and coaches appreciated his skill level. He was a natural and it was the best part-time job he could ever ask for.

"Santiago, let's go out?" asked Dai.

"There's a game tomorrow, I have to wake up at six o'clock and take the train."

"It's been a long time since the three of us have gone out together," added Kan.

"Okay, Kan the Man, since it's your birthday . . . I'm in."

Santiago agreed to only an hour since he would have to wake up early the next day. The three musketeers walked into the bar. It was a full house, the music vibrating, as people were dancing. Most were Japanese, but two Westerners were spotted.

"Can you help us?" asked Kan.

"Help you what?" asked Santiago.

"Your English is much better than ours . . ."

Santiago approached the two girls, "Hey, are you having a good time?"

The girls smiled in relief.

"Where are you from?"

"We're from Manhattan," the girls replied.

"Today is my friend's birthday, would you like to join us?" It was rather forward of Santiago, but he did it for Kan.

"Sure, let's go dance," said one of the girls. Kan and Dai headed to the dance floor.

Santiago locked eyes with a girl, but two seconds later lost her in the crowd. He was so focused on the Westerners that he had missed an opportunity. He decided to get a drink for Kan, meanwhile scanning the dance floor for the girl. She was different.

Santiago dreamt about the girl that night. She was petite, with short hair, and had a cute smile. She had glasses and an alternative style. He hoped that she was local and that they would cross paths again someday, but Kyoto is a big city.

He sent her good thoughts and imagined scenarios of when they would meet again. But he had to focus on the game the next day and reviewed plays in his head. Although he was a referee, he often thought like a coach. He was born to play fútbol and it would be a shame if he didn't use this talent.

In that sense, Santiago was wise beyond his years. Most men in their twenties are experimenting, obsessed with sports, and partying every weekend. Santiago was mature for his age due to the loss of his mother. He was very disciplined and more "Japanese" than his roommates.

It was similar to Asha's feelings of being "Indian," and Santiago often thought of Asha when he was abroad. He missed her teachings and her nurture. She was in fact, his new mother.

One night, the three men decided to barbeque. Santiago had learned how to marinate from Sofia. "The secret is in the onions," he explained to his roommates. Kan and Dai were familiar with Teriyaki, but not the concept of barbeque.

Santiago loved meat, and Asha and Ilya had kept a mainly vegetarian home, so it had been years since he had enjoyed such a feast. They invited a few friends over and started the grill. Santiago ran to the local market to find rosemary and onions. He ran to the store, because he was excited to barbeque with his friends. As he entered the store, he found the onions quickly, but they did not carry herbs. He would have to take the metro to an international market. It was one stop away, so it was okay with him.

Santiago entered, "Excuse me, do you have cilantro and rosemary?" he asked.

The gentleman walked him over to the appropriate section of the market. We are out of rosemary, but let me check the stock. Santiago was growing impatient, until a girl walked into his aisle. It was as if time had stopped. Santiago felt weak in his knees. Was it fate? It was the girl from the bar.

"*Santiago no kon'nichiwa, watashi wa,*" he said to the girl. Santiago had to introduce himself to her. Aiko was her name, and she vaguely remembered him.

"Would you like to join us for a dinner party?" asked Santiago. He was as bold as his father.

"Maybe another time," said Aiko. They talked for thirty minutes and agreed to meet the following weekend.

Aiko was a Buddhist. She lived simply and reminded him of Asha. She had an inner light that glowed. Aiko and Asha were spiritual beings. Santiago wanted to be spiritual as well, but was restless inside. He could not free his mind.

As the Baal Shem Tov (Jewish mystical rabbi) once said, "From every human being there rises a light . . . and when two souls are destined to find one another, their two streams of light flow together and a single brighter light goes forth from their united being." Aiko tried to help him, but he was too neurotic. Maybe Aiko was his opposite, but she definitely calmed him down. They fit together nicely. In fact, they became inseparable, which was a bit of a nuisance to his roommates. They talked about a future together, but only after Aiko finished business school.

Although Santiago was content with Aiko, he started to feel homesick. He was bound by a two-year contract at work. He hadn't visited California in over a year and planned to visit in the summer. Kan and Dai wanted to go with him.

Kan had been dating Emily (the girl from the bar). They hit it off on the dance floor and she had moved to the same apartment complex. Her family lived in Napa Valley in California, and she wanted them to meet Kan. Dai was still obsessed with Russian women. His Russian improved and he wanted to practice with Ilya. He chatted with some girls online, but they lived in Russia. One girl, Katya, had promised to visit him in Japan, but she never came. Santiago promised to introduce him to some nice Russian girls if he ever visited San Francisco. Dai was actually looking for jobs in California, and there was a possibility that his company would allow a transfer.

Santiago and Dai discussed moving within the year, but Kan wanted to be close to his family in Kyoto. Kan was willing to meet Emily's parents in Napa, but not to relocate. Kan was always dating girls, but never ready to settle down. But Santiago was ready to bring Aiko home. Most girls like to be close to their families, but Aiko kept an open mind. She decided to look for placements in California, and was offered a two-year contract position at Apple headquarters in Cupertino, California. It wasn't San Francisco, but it was at least the Bay Area. Apple needed an immediate answer, and Aiko impulsively accepted.

Tickets were purchased, bags packed, and Aiko and Santiago were on the move. He knew his mother Sofia would be happy for him that he found love. Aiko's family did not interfere with her decision, and were especially supportive of her internship at Apple. She was ready to meet Santiago's family, start a new position, and live in a new country.

~11~

Art of Seva

Two years before, Santiago had made a similar transition as Aiko was now making. Although he did have family to support him, he still had felt alone initially. The loss of his mother was very difficult for him. It was in Aiko that he began to find himself again. He wanted to be there for her emotionally, physically, and spiritually.

Aiko loved San Francisco, its art and nature. She took the time to get to know the city and they found a nice apartment in Japantown. There was a peace pagoda in the park as well as jazz clubs and a plethora of restaurants. Santiago and Aiko especially enjoyed the neighborhood kabuki and saunas.

As in Japan, she had to wake up early to take the train to work, and was home in time to cook dinner for Santiago. On the weekends, they cooked together. The local markets offered Japanese products, but the sushi wasn't the same. In general, they avoided Japanese restaurants since they were able to cook the same dishes at home.

They loved to hike and often went to the Santa Cruz Mountains. In fact, they had a favorite beach along the Pacific Highway. It was hidden. Its access was also difficult. One would need to hike down a long and windy dirt path down a cliff. Aiko had a special rock that she meditated on every time they visited the beach. Santiago loved the water and would swim in the ocean. There were never many people on the beach, just a few students from University of California Santa Cruz. One day, as Aiko was in deep meditation, Santiago was busy writing something in the sand.

She awoke from meditation, the sun was bright, and she started to read his message, "Will you . . ." she couldn't quite make out the words from her angle. So, she got up and read the full message, "Will you marry me?" Aiko jumped for joy. Santiago was on one knee and asked for her hand in marriage. He told her that before he left Japan, he called her father and asked permission. Both sets of parents gave their blessings to the couple. Life was bliss.

Aiko wanted to tell all the girls on the beach, but there was only one. Her cell phone had no reception either, so she would have to wait to tell her family and friends about her engagement. This was their time. Santiago and Aiko enjoyed the moment. "Can we get married in a Buddhist temple?" she asked. "Of course," said Santiago, "I would love that, too."

Everything was in place, their jobs, marriage, and they were happy. They found a private Buddhist temple in San Francisco and a priest to officiate the ceremony. Aiko's parents flew in from Kyoto, Japan. Only family and a few friends were invited. The couple wanted an intimate event, nothing too extravagant.

Ilya and Asha had been saving for a day like this and instead of paying for a lavish wedding, they decided to help toward a down payment for their first home. Ilya and Asha loved Aiko and were happy to see Santiago settled. Asha would like to feel she had had some influence on his decision. The two were very similar and she was truly happy for him.

As years went by, Aiko started to change. It seemed the only thing important to Aiko was herself and Santiago. She was also very close to her family in Japan, and was focused on moving back one day. She realized she could not get too close to Santiago's parents because she wanted Santiago to move to Japan eventually and it would be easier to do that if the two of them were not close to Santiago's parents. Suddenly, their calendar was full and they had little time for Ilya or Asha. Asha was a giver and spoiled Aiko, but there was no reciprocity. And when there is no reciprocity in a relationship, it breaks. Although Aiko's behavior hurt Asha, she would always love her son. Unfortunately, Santiago was caught in the middle.

He knew he could not ignore his family, but his new priority was to make his wife happy. So, Asha distanced herself from Aiko, but maintained the lines of communication with Santiago. Ilya and Asha did not want to interfere in their relationship. Aiko and Santiago ultimately agreed to settle in Japan. As soon as Aiko's Apple contract was completed, they would relocate to Japan and start a family.

Asha re-channeled her energy into community service. Asha contacted her uncle in India. He ensured that her monetary donations were spent properly. He sent her photos of the rooms built and the bicycles that she sent to the children. At times, she thought about quitting her job and moving to India to help the orphans. But she came to realize that her fundraising efforts in the U.S. would have a greater impact on the orphans.

The orphanage became her baby as if part of some divine plan. She did not get credit or tax breaks; it was something she wanted to do for herself. She decided to develop a curriculum in English. The syllabus would include tools that would help these children be competitive in the Indian workforce. She wanted to increase literacy rates and break the cycle of poverty, one child at a time. She would raise funds through international nonprofit organizations. It was also a project that she and Ilya could work on together. Although Ilya did not have the same ties to India, he too was a social worker at heart.

After Ilya's visit to the orphanage, his interest in social enterprises swelled. Ilya focused on sustainability. It was keen of Asha to send bicycles to the orphans, but what about maintenance? Should she have also sent locks so the bikes would not get stolen? How would the children address flat tires? Ilya took it upon himself to send locks and train the children on maintenance of the bicycles. Asha had a list of projects in the pipeline—waste management and recycling interested Ilya most. He worked on monitoring the effectiveness of Asha's interventions through surveys and collection of qualitative data.

To affect true transformation is a multi-dimensional effort. It took partnerships with educators, social workers, physicians, hospitals, engineers, and mental health professionals to really change the disposition of the orphanage and the lives of the children. Asha learned that many of the children were found in trash bins or on the beach. Social workers would collect the children, take them to hospitals to have health screenings, and then house them.

Asha's father was a member of the Sevaks, a group who believed in a similar mission as Asha. *Seva* is a Sanskrit word that refers to volunteer work, selfless service or work offered to God. But Asha did not want to create a foundation, nor did she have the infrastructure or funds like the Sevaks, so she decided to work directly with her uncle in India. Asha gained pleasure by helping others.

Ilya enjoyed helping Asha, but he felt pulled in many directions. Although he embraced his new multicultural family— Indian wife, South American son, and Japanese daughter-in-law— he began to struggle with his Jewish identity. Part of him wanted to run to Israel and join the army, and part of him wanted to stay in California. Ilya was holding on to his Jewish traditions and still wanted a HinJew life.

During the high holidays, he became especially close with his family. It was okay that Asha did not attend every service in the temple. Asha and Santiago participated in the major Jewish holidays, but not all. Ilya often went alone to see his family. He needed to do it for himself. Religion is for you, not others. As the Sufi proverb goes, "I searched for God and found only myself. I searched for myself and found only God."

~12~

Bellafigura

One summer day, a letter from Texas arrived in the mail. Asha hadn't heard from Texas since her last business trip. The envelope was small and there was no return address, just the name Moradi. Was it from Farshad's family? She started to fear that something was wrong. She opened the letter quickly and it was from Nina. Asha was happy to get a handwritten letter on perforated stationary:

> Dear Asha,
>
> I hope this letter finds you and you're well. I've wanted to reconnect with you for some time now; can I come pay you a visit? Please call me as soon as you can.
>
> Love,
> Nina

Nina did not leave a telephone number, so Asha contacted Sarah for it. Asha did not have many friends, but the few she had were lifelong friends. Girlfriends always seem to stay by your side, and Asha wanted to be a good friend to Nina. For some reason, she always felt a bond with Nina. Asha decided to call her the following weekend.

Nina was in trouble. She divorced her husband, which was a good thing. But all her friends were her husband's and she was alone. Often a divorce is difficult for friends since they feel forced to choose sides. She sought out the many relationships that had departed from her life in earlier years. It was a clean slate now, and Asha was the first person she contacted.

Asha purchased a plane ticket for Nina since she did not have money. Asha and Ilya's home was becoming a safe house. Their house was located on a street lined with palm trees. Many visitors came and went, and they had little privacy.

Asha's parents planned to live in a retirement community with people their age, and Arun was settled in the East Coast, so her friends became her major support system. Nina stayed a week with Asha. It turns out she was a fantastic cook and she loved to feed people. Ilya and Asha never ate so much in their lives. It was a dinner party every day of the week. Asha and Nina would chat all night and often fell asleep on the couch. It was the sister she had always wanted. Asha was blessed.

"Nina, you have to move here," said Asha.

"I've been looking at new jobs in Florida to promote my art, maybe I can look into San Francisco?" thought Nina.

"You can always stay with us if you need to," reassured Asha.

"Thanks, you've been so kind already," stated Nina.

Asha needed Nina, too. They seemed to be turning into their mothers. Asha would make the tea, Nina would cook, and they would chat for hours. Just like the Indian aunties Asha grew up with during her childhood. Somehow, Asha was part of the formula again. She wanted to help Nina, but had to resume her role as a wife, too. She felt lucky to have a close girlfriend like Nina. Her heart was full again.

Nina held odd jobs to support her passion for art and sculpture. Her art evoked the struggle of animal rights. It was a silent protest. Nina was vegan and did not eat anything with a face. Asha was also vegetarian, but for different reasons. Nina's sculptures reflected her views, but she needed to find herself on the market. She wanted to reach a global audience, not just animal rights activists.

Nina entered her pieces into local art shows. Night after night, she promoted her art. She learned how to create a website and posted her pieces online. The art was bold and colorful, and she met artists with connections. She was in the circle. She attended events every weekend and painted for days. It took patience, but she knew she would get there. One buyer was willing to mass-produce her pieces in China for a percentage of her company. But Nina did not have a label or a company; she would have to become an entrepreneur overnight.

She credited her success to Asha. Asha was her muse. In fact, she wanted to incorporate her name into the brand and called it *Nisha* (Nina + Asha) *Arts*. Although she was far away in Washington D.C., Nina would always be grateful to Asha. She looked to her for inspiration and Asha delivered. *Nisha Arts* became nationally recognized, from New York to Los Angeles. Eventually, she hired a company to manage Internet sales and finances. Yes, she could move to Paris or Rome to improve her European sales, but she decided to stay in the U.S.

Nisha Arts flourished. Her best-seller was a Venetian lampshade she designed for which she traveled to India to dye silks and to Italy for manufacture. She established connections in Rome and Milan, and bought a small factory north of Venice in Murano. The only way to her factory was by boat to a series of islands linked by bridges. Murano is known for glass blowing, particularly lampworking. It was a place she could be creative and her art came to life. She lived in a bubble and could only visit for a month at a time.

The art circle consumed Nina. It was exhausting, but in order to sell art, it was compulsory. Orders were coming in and business was booming. Despite a minor lawsuit filed by a delivery company, *Nisha Arts* was a great success. Her debt subsided and she was able to help her parents financially. Her parents could retire early and close down the restaurant. Farshad had been a physician in Iran, but he had difficulty with bedside manner due to his accent and could never pass the oral exams in the U.S. He had never wanted to open a restaurant. But he was able to provide for his family through his restaurant businesses. Nina learned the trade by osmosis.

The only thing missing in her life was a relationship. *Nisha Arts* was her husband, her home, and her life. She joined a local Church and made new friends. It was a good support group and kept her grounded. For the moment, she was content with her friends and

Nisha Arts. She sold Venetian lampshades to famous people, but had no desire to become famous. In ten years, she could sell the business and retire. Asha and Nina had had very different paths in life, but they had always been striving for the same destination.

Asha also reclaimed her happiness. At the age of thirty-five, she found balance in her HinJew life. She was a good wife to Ilya, a caring mother to Santiago, and at peace with herself. Her only unfulfilled wish was to have a child of her own and that was in God's hands.

GLOSSARY

Glossary

Aagami	Future karma
Agni	Fire
Ajna	Brow
Anahata	Heart
Artha	Wealth
Ashrivad	Blessings
Baal Shem Tov	Mystical Rabbi
Bella	Beautiful
Benvenuti	Welcome in Italian
Bienvenidos	Welcome in Spanish
Bible Belt	South-central US
Binah	Understanding
Bollywood	India's Hollywood
Buongiorno	Good morning
Chakra	Energy Center
Chanukah	Jewish festival of lights
Chessed	Kindness
Chochmah	Wisdom
Chuppah	Canopy in Hebrew
Crème brûlée	Custard topped with caramel
Daat	Knowledge
Dharma	Duty
Diwali	Hindu festival of lights
Dolares	Dollars
Está bien	Okay; good
Fútbol	Soccer
Ganesha Puja	Prayer to worship Lord Ganesha
Gevurah	Strength
Granthi Bandhan	Bride's & groom's scarves tied together
Gunas	Moods

Glossary

Haatha Ganthi	Placement of bride's hands into Groom's
Habibti	My beloved
Hamsa	Palm-shaped amulet
Hasidic	Orthodox Judaism
Havan	Prayer to the Lord of Fire
Hiragana	Japanese syllabry
Hod	Splendor
Hola	Hello in Spanish
Holi	Hindu festival of Spring
Induska	Indian female in Russian
Jai Mala	Garland exchange
Kabbalah	Jewish esoteric teachings
Kabuki	Japanese dance-drama
Kama	Love; desire
Kansarbhoj	Bride & groom feed one another sweets
Kanyadaan	Parents give the bride away for marriage
Karma	Action; deed
Katakana	Japanese writing system
Ketubah	Jewish marriage contract
Kiddushin	Sanctification; dedication
Kolkata	Indian city formally known as Calcutta
Kon'nichiwa	Japanese greeting
Kriyamana	Instant karma
Kurti	Indian shirt; top
La crème	Cream
Ladki	Girl in Hindi
Lassi	Indian yogurt drink
Latke	Potato pancakes
Lajja Vastra	Groom's parents offer bride a gift

Glossary

Lunfardo	Argentinean dialect
Lungi	Garment wrapped around the waist
Malchut	Kingship
Mandap	Canopy in Hindi
Mangal Phera	To walk around the fire seven times
Manipura	Solar Plexus
Mantra	A repeated word or phrase
Masha'Allah	Appreciation; joy
Mazel Tov	Congratulations
Mercato	Market
Middot	Emotions
Moksha	Salvation
Muladhara	Root
Mumbai	Indian city formally known as Bombay
Namaste	Indian greeting; salutation
Netzach	Victory
Oui	Yes in French
Paella	Valencian rice dish
Por favor	Please
Puja	Religious ritual
Praarabdha	Fruitful karma
Quatre Saisons	Four Seasons
Rabbi	Jewish priest
Rajogun	Passion
Reiki	Japanese spiritual practice
Rosh Hashanah	Jewish New Year
Sahasrara	Crown; top of head
Sala Bidha	Brother-in-law pat on the back
Sanchita	Total karma

Glossary

Sangria	Spanish wine punch
Saptapadi	Seven steps
Sari	Indian cloth draped over the body
Sarong	Long fabric wrapped around waist
Satogun	Purity
Sechel	Intellect
Sefirot	Enumerations of Kabbalah
Señor	Mister
Señorita	Miss
Seva	Self-less service; volunteer work
Sheva Brachot	Seven blessings
Shiksa	Non-Jewish woman
Sí	Yes in Spanish
Simcha	Joy
Sindoor	Vermillion
Swadhisthana	Sacral
Tamogun	Inertia
Tiferet	Beauty
Torah	Jewish Bible
Var Agaman	Groom's welcome
Veinte	Twenty
Vishudda	Throat
Yesod	Foundation
Yichud	Seclusion
Yom Kippur	Jewish Day of Atonement